ALSO BY JESSI THIND

Lions of the Sea
Lions on the Western Front
The Singer, The Player, The Bard and his Dragon
84

Saragarhi

© Copyright 2007 Jessi Thind.
All rights reserved. No part of this publication may be reproduced, stored in a retrieval system, or transmitted, in any form or by any means, electronic, mechanical, photocopying, recording, or otherwise, without the written prior permission of the author.

This is a work of fiction based on a true story. Names, characters, places and incidents are either the product of the author's imagination or are used fictitiously. Any resemblance to actual persons, living or dead, events or locales is entirely coincidental.

Note for Librarians: A cataloguing record for this book is available from Library and Archives Canada at www.collectionscanada.ca/amicus/index-e.html
ISBN 978-1-4251-2761-9

Printed in Victoria, BC, Canada. Printed on paper with minimum 30% recycled fibre.
Trafford's print shop runs on "green energy" from solar, wind and other environmentally-friendly power sources.

Offices in Canada, USA, Ireland and UK

Book sales for North America and international:
Trafford Publishing, 6E–2333 Government St.,
Victoria, BC V8T 4P4 CANADA
phone 250 383 6864 (toll-free 1 888 232 4444)
fax 250 383 6804; email to orders@trafford.com

Book sales in Europe:
Trafford Publishing (UK) Limited, 9 Park End Street, 2nd Floor
Oxford, UK OX1 1HH UNITED KINGDOM
phone +44 (0)1865 722 113 (local rate 0845 230 9601)
facsimile +44 (0)1865 722 868; info.uk@trafford.com

Order online at:
trafford.com/07-0950

10 9 8 7 6 5 4 3 2 1

Saragarhi

Dedicated to my dear father. Thank you for having shared your life with me. Thank you for having always reminded me of my essence, my roots, and my identity, for having passed down the torch of our experiences and our history at the dinner table, in the car, at cafés. Thank you, for all those extraordinary stories, like this one, that I would have otherwise never heard about or read about. Thank you for having kept the sacred fire of our history burning strong and fierce in me. Thank you.

Saragarhi

September 12, 1897.

At the northernmost border of British India several forts guard the Queen's frontier from tribal invasions. For weeks, tribal chiefs and Afghan militia have attempted without success to defeat the 36th Sikh Battalion garrisoned at Fort Gulistan and Fort Lockhart. Nestled between these two forts is a small, strategic signaling outpost used to relay messages between officers at Gulistan and Lockhart. There, at Saragarhi, Havildar Ishar Singh and twenty of his men wake up before dawn and begin their morning prayers...

Fluttering through the early morning dark, a butterfly perched on a crisp, dry shrub, opening and closing radiant blue and white wings. It sat before the ancient-looking outpost, as though captivated by the sounds of morning prayer. Silhouetted against the dawn, a buzzard circled above the rocky frontier, searching forthe remnants of battle and the promise of a feast. Beyond the distant mountains, the sky bloomed red and orange and gradually dimmed the late-night stars. The night before, soldiers across the frontier had admired the stars for hours on end, relieving their eyes from the somber colors of the war-torn surroundings. While the stars brought their eyes temporary relief, each soldier had gazed upon them in silent dread of the day to come. Clear night skies and bright stars promised a day of impossible sun and unforgiving heat - heat so fierce the air would shimmer, and every breath would assail the lungs like fire. But such unforgiving days were not uncommon on the frontier. Soldiers often collapsed and died of heat exhaustion. But the morning air was still cool.

    Prayers stopped and the world went silent for a moment. The butterfly closed its delicate wings and remained still like a tiny statue. When the prayers continued, the butterfly came to life and sprang off the shrub. It took to the sky and made its way to the source of sounds that hypnotized it. It fluttered over rocky, inhospitable land searching for a blade of grass or shrub on which to alight. Finding no suitable place to rest, it continued on toward the outpost as the sound of prayers grew louder.

    When the butterfly finally reached the outpost, it found a few bushes by the wall and, after inspection, settled on a long, shriveled leaf where it continued its meditation. In the deep red sky above, two dark scavengers circled for a long moment, then soared over the ridge and disappeared behind a hill.

Jessi Thind's Saragarhi

Once again, the world fell silent and the butterfly took to the sky. It fluttered along a stone wall that stood the height of four men. The butterfly followed the wall to a thick, wooden door - the outpost's only entrance. It hovered near the rotten door for a moment, then perched on a nearby shrub and spread its wings.

Inside the outpost, Sikh soldiers of the 36th Battalion, clad in their distinct regimental uniforms-a fleece-lined poshteen over khaki kurta, a thick leather belt with two pouches, a canteen, a mess kit, a kirpan, and a sharp quoit over a perfectly-tied, khaki turban-stood facing their havildar, Ishar Singh. He began the final prayers, Ardas, reminding each soldier of his origins, his history, his beloved ancestors-how they had defended the poor, fought against tyranny, and sacrificed their lives for their faith. At the end of these powerful words, they bent down on one knee and bowed their heads. A moment later, they were on their feet again, breathing the cool morning air. After a short meditative silence, Ishar said a few more words. Then, when he concluded the prayers, the regiment called out in unison:

"Sat Sri Akal!"

True is the Timeless Being.

At this, the butterfly sprang, fluttered about the wall, and found an opening. Through a rifle gun slit, the butterfly entered the outpost and fluttered above twenty men standing at attention. Ishar circled and carefully inspected each man. His sharp, trained eyes examined individual uniforms and turbans to make sure they were perfect. When he was satisfied, he gave his men their tasks. So began a new day on the frontier.

Big, black, dusty ants scurried quickly over the earthen ground searching for food. Gurmukh watched as one ant kept bumping into his boot. He watched it with curiosity and admiration. He observed the ant as it paused for a moment to problem-solve. It scampered left, then right, then paused again, and seemed to stare at the boot with a measure of indignation. Gurmukh smiled and watched with amusement as the ant began a slow, dedicated climb over his boot, as if it were scaling a mountain. He watched the ant scurry across the leather surface, then down the side. His eyes lingered on the tiny insect as it journeyed toward the barrack room, where other ants gathered in great numbers, busy and excited over some potato skins and lentils that had not been properly disposed.

Gurmukh gazed at the ant for a thoughtful moment. He wondered if this ant even knew he was there; he wondered if ants knew human beings existed. Could such a tiny creature see or grasp the concept of a living thing a million times its size, weight, and strength? He watched the ant until it disappeared into the barrack room, then turned his attention to a small leather case in his hand. His heliograph.

Gurmukh, a medium build, soft-spoken man, was the quickest and most accomplished signaler in his regiment; he could relay almost any message using light. He opened the straps of the leather case and pulled out a heliograph. He gazed at his instrument, then raised his eyes to the lightening sky. He looked back to his heliograph, sat down on a stack of burlap sandbags and began to hum his family protection shabad, reflecting the words against the shadowy wall of the outpost with his instrument.

"Jaa thoo merai val hai thaa ki-aa muhushundhaa."

When you are on my side, Lord, what do I need to worry about?

Suddenly, Sepoy Buta Singh came up to Gurmukh. He was a

short, thin man with dreamy eyes and an absent air about him. He seemed to be in a perpetual daze, meditating on how to improve his life, his surroundings, and his world. He listened to the tune Gurmukh hummed and instantly recognized it. "Always the same shabad with you," he said, shaking his head with a faint smile. "Have you not learned any other?"

Gurmukh turned to Buta and said, "My father used to sing it to me, and his father used to sing it to him. It's my family protection shabad. It strengthens me. It builds me and carries me to a place only such powerful words can take a person."

Buta took a step closer. "There are other shabads. Many others powerful words. You could conceivably try another." He sighed faintly and added "So many beautiful shabads available to you, and yet…always…always…Jaa thoo merai val hai thaa ki-aa muhushunda. Don't you ever tire of them?"

"Tire?" Gurmukh laughed. "Of course not. How does one tire of such beautiful words?" He repeated the shabad to himself, pausing after each verse, appreciating and absorbing the meaning. When he finished, he paused, looked up to Buta, and asked, "Don't you have a family protection shabad, Butaji?"

Buta shook his head in reply. A hint of disappointment flashed in his eyes. When he didn't say anymore, Gurmukh questioned, "No?"

"No."

Gurmukh sighed with sadness for him and turned his attention back to his heliograph. "I thought everyone had a family protection shabad. At least that is what my father told me." He paused a moment and turned to Buta. "My fatherused to say that you can take any verse from the Guru Granth Sahib, and it will fill your heart with such strength, such power, such truth, that you can overcome any situation." He gazed up at the steadily brightening sky and knew it would be another unbearably hot day. He turned back to Buta. "It was my grandfather's protection shabad. It was my father's protection shabad. And now, it is my protection shabad."

Buta took a step closer and sat beside him. After a moment, he asked, "How come I don't have a family protection shabad?"

Gurmukh shrugged. "I don't know. Why ask me? Ask your father."

A short silence followed. Buta stroked his beard pensively. He stopped suddenly, turned to Gurmukh and asked, "Can I choose any shabad?"

Gurmukh thought about this a moment as he observed the cloudless sky. "I don't know, I suppose you could. But usually, they are passed down."

"I want a family protection shabad."

"You should have one."

"Can I adopt your family protection shabad?"

"As you wish, Butaji. No one has ownership over shabads. No one."

"Because I've thought over the words, and they mean a lot to me, and I think that it is true. If Waheguru is on your side, what do you have to worry about?"

Instantly, Gurmukh answered, "Nothing,"

"Exactly. Nothing."

Gurmukh peered up at the sky. It was bluer and brighter now, and in the distance he could see silhouettes of buzzards circling. Buta followed his gaze and knew what his friend was thinking.

"Yes," Buta said, "the sun has already begun its slow torture on us."

Gurmukh nodded.

"At least," Buta continued, "you won't have to worry about the sun hiding in the clouds. It's the clearest sky I have ever seen." He gasped. "Ahh! It will be a sunny day, and you'll be able to play with your friends at Lockhart without interference."

"Play?" Gurmukh questioned, then shot him a searing look. "It's hardly play being cooped up in a tower flashing messages all day."

"At least you do something challenging," Buta said. "What do I do? Clean latrines, dig useless holes, fill bags, polish my rifle over and over again…and wait…wait…for something that will never happen." His gaze swept the outpost. "Not here, anyway. Nothing happens here. Who would attack such an insignificant place? What respectable chief would attack Saragarhi? What honor is there in attacking a mud-box way out in the middle of nowhere?"

Gurmukh thought it over. At last he said, "Up to now the Afghans and Pathans have been deeply humiliated in every attempt they have made on Gulistan. Perhaps attacking Saragarhi would help their morale."

Buta considered this a moment. "Perhaps. Yes, perhaps. But, if that were in fact so, the lieutenant would have left more men here, more ammunition, more provisions. He knows as well as I do…there is nothing here for the Afghans." He sighed and declared, "We are the claws, the teeth, the strength, and the roar of the Empire, and I feel cheated. I feel cheated, Brother. This box is no place for a lion. I should be with my pride. I should be with the rest of my brothers at Gulistan, where they will need me."

"I need you."

"You?"

"Sure."

Gurmukh turned slightly and indicated the signaling tower just above the barrack room. "What if I were to suddenly collapse up there?"

"I suppose."

"You see? You are needed."

"Yes, I see."

Buta let out a sigh. "But I still feel cheated," he said. "I mean, what stories will I have for my children and my grandchildren in the future?"

"Is that it, then?" Gurmukh shook his head, almost in disbelief. "Is that what you are about? What stories you will be able to tell your grandchildren?"

Buta shrugged slightly. "Well, I'm not quite sure what I could tell them."

Gurmukh laughed. He looked to the sky, then turned to Buta.

"You could tell them that you did your duty. That you did your duty without wishing you could do someone else's. That you did your duty without wishing you were somewhere else. And doing your duty, Butaji, is always enough. Always."

Buta nodded. "Yes, I know you are right. I just wish there'd be more to it than hanging around some dilapidated box. That's all. I wish I could be where this--" He indicated his forehead with his forefinger. "--mind would be put to better use, where there will be action and grandchildren-worthy stories."

Gurmukh warned, "Be careful what you wish for."

Buta appeared to dismiss the warning. He continued. "They will attack again, and I will have to tell my grandchildren what I saw from here. That I was witness to a great story, and not part of it."

A long silenced followed, and Gurmukh, sensing food was almost ready, packed up his heliograph. Hungry men gathered around the two cooks as they prepared daal and rotis for the regiment. Gentle streams of smoke rose into the sky and disappeared. A faint splash of clove and cardamom spiced the air.

Buta sat with his head down. A sudden idea came to him. "I tell you what we need," he said, breaking the silence. "I've been thinking, and I have come up with something incredible. Something extraordinary. Something that will amaze, daze, and confound you."

Buta often spoke of things that his mind constructed on the spur of the moment. He enjoyed nothing more than to read about new processes and technologies in the world of science, which he wrote about in a journal he kept in his mess kit. In this journal, he kept notes and observations as they came to him, for he felt if he stopped writing, he would dam and disconnect the river of his thoughts from a boundless ocean of ideas. The source. Recording all that came to him without judgment or criticism was his way of keeping the river flowing, beautifully, powerfully, and endlessly. He beamed at Gurmukh with bright eyes.

"I have been thinking about this sun, you see, and I've been thinking...what if we made spectacles that protected our eyes from its brightness. Spectacles that protected the eyes from the brightness and heat."

He waited for Gurmukh's reaction, but received none.

"Spectacles that were slightly darkened so that the darkness would absorb some of the light before it hits your eyes. And I assure you, glass can be darkened with smoke. I have read about it."

"It's a ridiculous idea," Gurmukh said flatly. "I am neither amazed, dazed, nor confounded. Protection from the sun? The sun? The sun is a menace, but it is of no real concern or consequence. Be concerned with the Pathans and Orkazi, not the sun."

"But think about it," Buta argued. "You wouldn't need to squint anymore. You wouldn't need to use your hand for shade anymore. And imagine, just imagine! You are in battle, and you are momentarily blinded, and in that brief moment of blindness, you are given the deathblow." Buta leaned backward almost imperially, and crossed his arms, his eyes grave and serious.

Unconvinced, Gurmukh said, "Then I would say that was your destiny. I would say that was the death that was written out for you long, long ago, by the same hand that had written that you would first be blinded by the sun."

Buta looked to an ant on the ground. He watched it for a moment, then turned back to Gurmukh. "What if it were your destiny to have those special lenses? And what if...what if it were my destiny to bring these spectacles into existence? What do you say to that?"

Gurmukh didn't hesitate. "Then you would do it," he said. "And there is nothing in this world that could stop you." He looked to the sky. "If a man is destined to drown, he will drown. He may try his best to avoid all the oceans, lakes, rivers and puddles, but he will drown, even if he only encounters a single drop of water."

Buta shook his head. "How can anyone drown in a drop of water?"

Gurmukh grimaced.

"It's just my way of saying that whatever Waheguru has planned for you, you will not escape, no matter how hard you try." Again, he looked to the sky. His voice lowered to a whisper. "One often meets his destiny on the very path he takes to avoid it."

Buta repeated this to himself. "So you mean to say..." He spoke slowly and thoughtfully. "...that we are here because we are destined to take a little rest?"

"No," Gurmukh's replied. "That is not what I mean to say. I mean to say that if we are meant to meet with the enemy, we will meet the enemy, whether we are at Lockhart, Gulistan, or here at Saragarhi. When it is time to meet the Guru, it is time to meet the Guru."

Buta repeated the words contemplatively. He turned toward the cooks and saw that food was being served. As he gazed at them, his eyes brightened with a thought. He turned back to Gurmukh. "I could call them Spectacles of the Sun."

"Terrible. That's a terrible name."

"Terrible? What's so terrible about it? Spectacles of the Sun."

"Too long," Gurmukh said. He considered the name for an instant. "How about just...Sun Spectacles?"

Buta repeated both names carefully, comparing and contrasting. "Yes," he said at last. "I like it better. Sun Spectacles. It is a much better name. Much better." He smiled wide at the name and nodded happily. "You will see - one day everyone will wear my Sun Spectacles." He paused to imagine the future. His eyes danced gloriously. "First, I will buy hundreds of spectacles. Second, I will darken all the lenses with smoke. Then, I will sell the idea to her Majesty, the Queen, and eventually all the Queen's men will have to wear these Sun Spectacles, and I will become a very, very wealthy man."

"Good," Gurmukh said with a little laugh. "Then I won't have to worry about losing my land and home to taxes."

"No," Buta said and shook his finger. "And neither will any of my brothers. And with the profit I will..." He thought a moment about what he would do with his wealth. "I will buy a hundred trees. And with those trees, I will build a boat, and with this boat I will travel the world a hundred times over."

Gurmukh looked deep into Buta's eyes and could imagine him in his boat sailing across the ocean.

"And with the rest of my wealth I will make other great things that will benefit the whole world. Things I will think about while on my sea voyage…like Red Beard. And like a pirate, you see, I will search the depths of my mind for great treasures…treasures of unsurpassed genius. Treasures that will help and inspire people. I will work with Waheguru, for others, on the sea. That is my destiny."

"You don't need a boat," Gurmukh observed. "You can search the depths of your mind without a boat."

Buta shook his head. "There is something about the water," he said, and paused to reflect. "There is something about the sound of water that relaxes the mind. It's been proven." He took a moment to gaze around at his surroundings. Then, remembering something an Irish soldier told him, he said, "You know, I met a soldier who said that this desert of sand and stone was once a mighty ocean of plankton and pearls. He told me that I shouldn't be surprised to find minnow and whale fossils in the ground." Buta extended his arms as though he were embracing the world. "Here! An ocean! Millions of years ago!"

He cherished the idea and took in a deep breath.

Gurmukh grinned at his friend's childlike excitement.

"No," Buta continued, "there is something about water that helps me relax my mind. And that is precisely why I will need a boat. To think. To think profoundly and clearly, so that I may dig deep into the depths of my mind for all the great treasures hidden in the dark caverns of eternity…treasures available to all who know how to get there."

"You could get lonely."
"I will bring all my friends!"
"You would tire of the water."
"I will bring a box of earth."

"You could starve."
"I'll bring plenty of rotis."
"What about walks?"
"What about them?"
"Long walks relax the mind. Clear the mind. Inspire. If you went on long walks, you wouldn't have to build a boat. You wouldn't have to go away for so long, and you wouldn't have to bring your friends, you could stay with them. You would save yourself headache, time, and money."

Buta sighed miserably. He didn't have an answer for this. He knew his friend was right. Long walks often relaxed and cleared his mind, inspired him. "Yes," he said, "I suppose you are right. I could go for long walks. It was just a dream, I suppose."

Gurmukh smiled. He could hear the pat of the rotis behind him, and his nostrils widened as he breathed in the rich aroma of ginger. "I'm hungry," he declared. He stood and turned toward the cooks.

Buta followed.

They took a step toward the breakfast congregation. Then, noticing the butterfly fluttering by them, they both stood still to admire it. "Imagine," Buta observed, "a tiny butterfly now flutters where a mighty whale once swam."

Gurmukh smiled broadly at this.
When the butterfly alighted on the wall and was still again, he fell back into step, singing a shabad in his mind. An ancient shabad, clear and powerful:

When You are on my side, Lord, what do I need to worry about?

You entrusted everything to me, when I became Your slave.

My wealth is inexhaustible, no matter how much I spend and consume.

The 8.4 million species of beings all work to serve me.

All these enemies have become my friends, and no one wishes me ill.

No one calls me to account, since the Lord is my forgiver.

I have become blissful, and I have found peace, meeting with the Guru, the Lord of the Universe.

All my affairs have been resolved, since You are pleased with me.

Strength and vitality returned to Gurmukh's awakening muscles as he swallowed a mouthful of liquid food. He tore another piece of roti and scooped it into his steamy, yellow daal. He sat on the ground beside Buta and two other soldiers. Buta chewed slowly, enjoying every flavor, passing comments and collecting opinions in his usual way. "We don't all need to be here," he said, gazing at two of his comrades, Daya and Jivan, for reactions. He looked more to Jivan. His comments were almost always harsher and far more provoking than Daya's, and they usually afforded him much more to write about in his journal. When Jivan wasn't memorizing passages out of the Guru Granth Sahib, he was exchanging confidences with Irish and Scottish soldiers. Through these foreign soldiers, he had learned a darker and more graphic history of those he served, a history of those who lived under tyranny, not those who dispensed it. It was through these soldiers that he experienced a far more oppressive face of the British. And now, he had gained a reputation amongst his friends as the professor. He was known for his long, one-sided, unapologetic tirades against British occupation in India and throughout the world.

Buta gazed into Jivan's deep, powerful eyesand waited. Nothing. After a moment, he turned his attention to Daya. He waited patiently. Nothing. Around them, soldiers were finishing breakfast. When neither responded, he added, "Only one or two of us need to be here, the rest should be at Gulistan where we are needed. Don't you think?"

Daya nodded his agreement, but didn't say anything. He had a thick, coarse beard, strong jaw, and sharp eyes that, combined with a rifle, never missed a target in practice or in battle. Unlike Jivan, he deeply respected the British. He respected their books and armies, their institutions and infrastructure, and he praised the order and laws he felt they had brought to India. Most of all, he respected and appreciated that he had equal status, that he was a British subject equal to all other subjects in the Empire, and that he was treated as such.

Buta added, "Maybe we are entitled to a little rest, a little contemplation."

Daya looked to Jivan and cringed when he saw him shaking his head at Buta's comment. He knew Jivan would, as always, offer his point-of-view, which was never lacking in breadth or pessimism.

Jivan was a tall, robust man who rarely smiled. Under his poshteen and kurta, lean, stone-like muscles bulged. His beard was long and perfectly groomed, and his turban, the picture of perfection, rose a few inches higher than any other. He stopped chewing. "Maybe," he said, gazing meditatively at the steam rising from his daal. "Maybe you are right. Maybe we are entitled to some rest and contemplation…but I don't think so…I mean, we might actually contemplate that we don't want to be here. We might contemplate that we don't want to die against an enemy over here on behalf of an even greater and far more abusive enemy overseas."

Daya sighed with annoyance at this observation. "No," he said flatly. "I do not think so. Maybe you would contemplate this, but not I. I will always choose the British over this enemy. Always. At least with the British I can own things and be treated as an equal. At least with the British, I can keep my religion, not that I would accept or have it any other way. But at least with the British our Gurdwaras still stand."

Buta smiled as his ears took in and his mind recorded every word.

"Only because the British need us now," Jivan countered. "Besides, they have other ways."

Daya ignored this. He turned to watch Ishar as he inspected

Jessi Thind's Saragarhi

the wooden door of the outpost, testing its strength and integrity. Then he turned back to Jivan. After a short silence, he said, "This enemy has no tolerance for others. This enemy has committed great acts of extinction against our people, our ancestors, and so many others. And why? Religious fanaticism. Intolerance. Because of their inability to live with others." He thought about the past for a moment. "You know," he continued, "this land once thrived with Buddhists and Buddhist monasteries."

He paused to let the words and images they created sink in.

In his mind, Buta could see a land replete with Buddhist monks and
monasteries.

"Where are the monasteries now?" Daya asked, turning to Buta and Gurmukh, then Jivan. "Where are the Buddhists now?" He waited for an answer. When none came, he answered for them, "Destroyed. Desecrated. Eliminated."

Jivan repeated the last three words to himself.

In his mind, Buta saw Buddhist monks being exterminated and monasteries being burnt down by leaders who used religion to justify their cruelty and destruction. Without realizing it, Daya's hand curled into a fist.

"This is our enemy. And it is their fanatical use of religion to justify their ends, and not their religion that I am against…that we are all against. It is and will forever be their intolerance and cruelty that I will forever raise my kirpan against. And the British…well, the British have nothing to do with why I fight or why I am here. In truth, it just works out that they stand with us against an old, old enemy. And I am grateful for it."

Buta nodded in agreement.

So did Gurmukh.

Daya's voice sharpened. "And like my ancestors," he said,

"I will die for what I believe in, for my beliefs, for my turban, for my kirpan, for my kara, for my right to proudly wear my blessed uniform-for my values, Jivan. For my values!. And my values are far closer to the British than the Afghan or the Pathan or the Orkazi…tribesmen who have, may I remind you, been invading and plundering our Punjab, and stealing our women and treasures for centuries."

Buta looked to Jivan. "He is right," he said evenly. "At least as a British subject I can own land."

Jivan sneered. "Land that was ours in the first place!"

Daya shook his head and raised a knowing finger to Jivan. "The truth of the matter is we can own land. We fight, we serve, and we may own land. We pay taxes, and we get equal status as British subjects. Equal. That doesn't sound like tyranny to me."

Jivan countered, "On paper. Paper equality. Paper equality with clauses in small print like the footnotes in their history books."

Daya turned to Jivan. "What is that supposed to mean, 'On paper'?"

Jivan took a bite of daal-roti, chewed, and swallowed. "It means what it means. The British are the masters of appearances. They are the masters of making things seem good and right on paper, but their paper is anything but good or right. They make themselves look fair and benevolent. Yet there is nothing fair or benevolent about them. Your equality is all a façade, and to think otherwise is only to fool yourself."

Daya sighed his irritation.

Jivan instantly responded to his sigh.

"No, it is true. British tyranny is one of endless politics and bureaucracy. They are tyrants with clauses and exceptions, which renders their tyranny polite, correct, and invisible. And when something is invisible, it is impossible to fight, defeat, challenge or change. Impossible unless you are a lawyer or an accountant, or some kind of master of numbers and letters."

"Don't you see?" Daya interjected, "that is exactly my point. We may become lawyers. We may become accountants. We may affect change."

"Do you really believe so?" Jivan asked, widening his eyes.
Daya fidgeted slightly. "And why wouldn't I?"
Jivan shook his head at his friend's innocence.

"Because the Anglo-Saxon is an evolved tyrant, Dayaji. That is why. Because everyone must play by his rules but him. His weapon is not the sword, but the pen. That is why, and that is what you should understand. We have status and equality now. Perhaps you are right. But for how long? Now they need us. They need us to protect and build their empire. Once we have spilled all our blood, once their language is spoken in every village of every country, once we are addicted to their way of life, they will leave our home. They will no longer need us."

Daya shook his head in obvious disaccord. "That won't happen," he said firmly. He looked hard into Jivan's eyes.

Jivan held his gaze. "No," he continued, "they will leave, and they will continue to control us from overseas. Only those who reject who they once were, only those who are properly Anglofied will be permitted to be lawyers, historians and accountants. They will continue to control us from overseas because they will control those who influence the masses. They will control those who wield the word like those who wield a sword, and with the mighty word, they will dominate us. You will see."

Daya instantly turned away from Jivan. He regarded the bright, deep blue sky. "That won't happen," he said in an uneasy tone. The mere thought of such a thing undermined his perception of the Empire and his future plans to move to the Dominion of Canada, where he had heard good farmland was being given to British subjects.

"It will happen," Jivan went on, almost in a whisper, as though his change in tone would hurt his comrade less. "And once they have used us, Dayaji, you will see. They will rob our children of their right to study numbers and letters. They will disenfranchise the Sikh in every part of the Empire, and, perhaps even right here, in our own home." He paused and wondered if he should go on. He had always spoken the truth, and he decided he wouldn't stop now, even if his words were upsetting those around him.

"They use the grand illusion of equality to entice us to fight their battles. But what do you suppose will happen when all these wars and battles have been fought and won? Do you suppose we will be permitted to keep our turban? Our kara? Our kirpan? Our sacred uniform?"

Every man stirred uncomfortably and let out a heavy breath of air. Buta wasn't sure what to think; he stroked his beard thoughtfully, not liking the idea of being disenfranchised in an Empire he fought for and defended, only because he was made to believe he was an equal subject. Nor did he want to entertain the idea that one day he would not be permitted to wear his religious uniform.

Daya turned to Jivan and said, "I don't believe that. I don't believe any of that. And when I have finished serving I will move to the Dominion of Canada."

"Where?" Buta asked.

"A dream," Daya answered. "A dream for any land-loving farmer of the British Empire."

"A dream for white subjects," Jivan corrected. "Not bearded brown subjects."

"You don't know that!"

Jivan took his last bite of daal-roti. "Understand this, and understand it well: you can die for the Englishman, but you cannot live with him. You can forget your Indian walk, and you can try to walk like an Englishman. You can forget your Indian talk, and talk like an Englishman. And you can even forget your bhangra, and waltz like an Englishman…but you will never live with him. Never."

Daya turned away once again. "I don't believe that," he said. "I don't believe it…"

"Believe the fairy tale if you wish, but I am much more realistic. And know that if you are, in fact, permitted to live in this part of the Empire, I would be very much surprised if you will ever be permitted land, or if your children will be allowed to learn letters and numbers. You can die for them, you can build for them, but you cannot live with them."

Jivan thought for a moment, then raised his voice slightly.

"The Anglo-Saxon will have you do all his menial tasks; he'll make you clean his latrines, he'll have you build his roads and his railways, and once you've built his country, he'll throw you a scrap of lard; he'll mention you as a footnote in his history, and then he'll dust you under the carpet of his civilization so that you and your children are no longer in his face to remind him of his laziness, of his tyranny, and of his unsurpassed intolerance."

Daya looked at him, aggravated.

Jivan didn't stop.

"So go to this place of abundant land, this dominion, but do not expect to be treated as an equal, for I am afraid you will be terribly disappointed. And let me just say this: The British aren't as close to the Sikh in values as you think. They are still very much backward in their thinking. How tolerant can they possibly be if their women aren't even considered persons, if their women are treated like children...like simple animals?"

Gurmukh looked up at him, surprised. "Is it true?"

Jivan nodded bleakly. "It is the truth. And such an attitude about their grandmothers, their mothers, their sisters, daughters, cousins, nieces, and aunts says a lot about who they are. Men and women are not equals to them, and that is as true as the sun in the sky. Women cannot be generals, they cannot be lawyers, they cannot be accountants, and in the Dominion of Canada, they are not even considered persons. I guarantee it."

He paused for a moment, then explained how he had come to know this.

"A man who interprets the law explained it to me. He said that in this part of the Empire women had no voting rights, and he said the reason women had no voting rights was because only a person could vote. Since women aren't 'persons,' they cannot vote. What equality can you expect from such a savage way of thinking? Be honest with yourself."

He let the words sink in. A hearty laugh from the cooks grabbed their attention for a moment. When the boisterous laughter receded to morning silence, Jivan turned to Daya. He went on:

"If they don't even consider their women people, do you think a bearded brown man with a turban will ever have the right to own land? Do you actually think they would value you more than their own women? Do you really believe they will give you that respect just because you are spilling your blood for them?"

Buta pulled at his beard. It was evident that he didn't want to hear any more. All this talk was boiling his blood more than the white sun in the sky, and he had more than enough fodder for his journal.

Daya turned away. "I don't believe that," he said quietly. "I don't believe any of that." He turned to Jivan. "It is merely something you heard in passing, and what you heard and the truth are two different things. And if that is how you feel about the Queen you serve, if that is how you truly feel, then why fight?"

Jivan shrugged. "What choice has this tyrant left us, Dayaji? To fight or to starve. Those are the options. But make no mistake: I have no illusions of who I am to the Anglo-Saxon, and if I fight, it is by your side, for my family, and it is, as you said, to protect my homeland from an ancient enemy. Not for the British."

A short silence followed. Gurmukh broke the tension with an absurd laugh. "I think when it is time to deal with the British, we will deal with the British."

All the men grunted their agreement.

Both Buta and Daya hoped Jivan would have nothing more to say on the issue.

"Yes," Jivan agreed. "Time will reveal the true face of the British. Now we are subjects. We are equal. We are told we may travel anywhere we wish in the Empire. We are needed, desperately needed. Let us see what happens when the fighting ends. Let us see how much they truly revere our kirpan, our turban, our uniform, our way of life. Let us see in a hundred years, when we are schoolmasters and accountants, if they will tolerate our uniform, or, if like our enemies of old, they will try to exterminate our way of life with their quill. Let us see if we are respected in the future as we are respected now. Let us see."

The sun was high now, and a buzzard soared over the outpost, sending a nameless wave of despair through every soldier's heart. At that moment Buta saw something tiny move in his peripheral. He turned round and his eyes sparkled when he saw the butterfly fluttering above a cluster of soldiers. After a reflective silence, he said, "It's a good sign, I think, to see a butterfly."

"No," Jivan corrected. "Not only for children." He watched the butterfly perch on a rifle, then continued: "There were people in a faraway land that once believed the butterfly was the ultimate symbol of the warrior. In battle, they wore butterfly breastplates, and they had colorful butterfly emblems on their weapons. And like the butterfly's life, they believed the warrior's life was short and painful, yet brilliant, beautiful, and full of glory."

Buta made a skeptical face and Jivan instantly reacted to his expression. "It is true," he said, raising a serious eyebrow. "They believed a warrior trained his whole life for one moment, the moment when he would bring incredible pride or shame to ancestors he believed were ever-present, always guiding him, protecting him, judging him."

He glanced around, as if searching for something or someone he could not see. Then he turned back to Daya, Gurmukh, and Buta. Feeling something he could not see or name, he continued:

"So strong were their beliefs and their reverence for their ancestors that they not only trained to fight with honor on the battlefield but learned how to die with honor against the enemy. They trained to resist pain and torture by learning special battle hymns that would raise their consciousness above their pain so that they would not disgrace their ancestors by surrendering."

He stopped, glancing at each soldier individually. He instantly noticed Buta's bright eyes, and he knew his imagination was constructing every image in perfect detail. He leaned toward him.

"Torture by the enemy was not feared, but accepted as fate. It was accepted as a sacred opportunity to prove ones ultimate worth as a warrior. To prove oneself worthy to be in the presence of one's ancestors."

Gurmukh nodded, listening intently.

"Torture was a sacred ceremony where both captor and captive had distinct roles to play. The captor had to carry out gruesome, yet compassionate acts against his prisoner. And during this ceremony, both prisoner and captor alike would face judgment from their ancestors. The captive had to endure all that was administered by his enemy, and to endure all this torture without issuing a single cry or whisper for mercy."

Jivan paused to consider what he would do in such a situation. He thought about all the Sikhs of a not-so-distant past who had gone through similar circumstances, who had endured senseless and indescribable torture in front of entire villages when they had refused to denounce their religion for another. He imagined Sikhs being tortured as they sang shabads or meditated on God's name to raise their consciousness above their pain. He could see Sikhs being thrashed, sawed, mangled, quartered, boiled, and even sewn tightly into the skin of a freshly slaughtered and gutted cow, then left in the sun to suffocate. He sighed heavily, his eyes glassy and distant.

"A warrior spent a lifetime preparing for this moment so that his passage to the next life would not be tainted by dishonor or cowardice. And so, as he was tortured in front of an entire village, instead of crying or begging for mercy, he sang louder and louder, lifting his spirit higher and higher above his pain."

Buta suddenly had an ardent desire to meet one of these warriors. "I respect these people," he said in a whisper, imagining a warrior claiming spiritual victory over his enemy through song. "I respect them greatly."

They all nodded in unison.

"A true warrior could endure torture for days," Jivan said. "And the torture would last until the victim had had enough and could no longer sing. And then, in front of everyone, the torturer would deliver an honorable deathblow and deliver the victim to his proud ancestors."

Gurmukh thought about this. He specifically thought about Jivan's choice of words. He didn't believe in the word 'victim'. After a moment, he said, "In a world ruled by death, the word 'victim' has no meaning. Either we are all victims, or none of us are."

"We are all victims," Buta said uncertainly.

Gurmukh shook his head. "No. None of us are."

Buta thought it over again. He nodded, agreeing with Gurmukh. In a world ruled by death, no one was a victim.

After a moment, the butterfly was before them and all eyes were hypnotized by it. They followed it as it made its way to the center of the courtyard, dancing up and down on an invisible current of wind. Then they watched helplessly as a sudden gust of wind slammed it across a splinter jutting out of the wooden door of the barrack room, where it tore a piece of its delicate wing and fell helplessly to the ground.

On seeing this, Buta instantly stood up. "That's not a good sign," he said.

"No, it's not," Gurmukh agreed. He watched Buta approach the butterfly with a hint of amusement. "Where are you going?"

"Maybe one of us will step on it. If I move it, maybe it will heal."

"Leave it!" Daya called out to him. "There is nothing you can do for it."

Jivan agreed. "Yes, leave it."

"What kind of soldiers are you that you wouldn't even help

a butterfly?" asked Buta.

They all regarded each other with half-smiles. Beautiful as it was, the others couldn't believe Buta's emotion over what was, to them, nothing more than an insect. It had occurred to Gurmukh that if butterflies looked like cockroaches, Buta would have let it bake in the sun. Perhaps he would have even gone out of his way to crush it rather than help it. He laughed at the thought and said, "There is nothing you can do for it. Like all of us, it has its destiny, and it seems that it is not meant to fly anymore."

Buta turned to him. "And how do you know my helping isn't part of Waheguru's plan?" he asked, rushing toward the fallen butterfly, which struggled desperately to fly away, but could only jerk and stagger in small circles.

Gurmukh knew his friend had a point. "I don't," he admitted. "Perhaps you are right. Perhaps it is part of the plan."

"If it is not meant to fly anymore, then nothing I do will change that."

Gurmukh agreed to this but said nothing.

Buta approached the dusty, crippled butterfly. He gasped when he observed the rip in its soft, delicate wing. He cupped the creature in his hands and told it that it would soon be better. Much better. Then his compassionate gaze swept the outpost for the perfect place where he felt it could heal out of harm's way.

Finally, he settled on a shaded area by the wall. He moved in gentle steps toward the spot, the whole while telling the butterfly it was going to be better soon. He placed it gently on the ground. Beside it, he made a tiny hole in the ground with his finger. He grabbed his canteen from his belt and filled the hole with water, telling the butterfly in a self-conscious whisper that, in this heat, it would need quite a bit of water for a strong and speedy recovery. He returned the canteen to his belt and turned to his comrades with a broad smile. Proud of his tiny act of compassion, he did not realize that he had unwittingly placed the butterfly next to an anthill.

Sitting by the wall, in the shade, Buta cringed as he polished his breech-loading rifle with a slightly oiled rag made from an old, discarded uniform. Behind him, the sun continued its climb above the distant mountains of Afghanistan. In front of him, a few soldiers plunged their bayonets into sandbags that were placed in such a way as to resemble eight-foot tribesmen. Nearby, Ishar hammered away at the door, reinforcing it with several beams he had found in the courtyard. One soldier suggested he had nothing to worry about, that he could fix the broken door another day. But something inside the havildar told him that the door had to be fixed and reinforced immediately. It was a strong intuition, which he obeyed, as he always did. Lives depended on it.

    Ishar was a tall, sturdy man with sharp eyes and an aura that commanded both respect and admiration from soldiers and civilians alike. He stood straight, made decisions quickly, and he always seemed ready for the unexpected. A highly esteemed havildar in the regiment, he was a great leader. And like most great leaders, he led by example and not by sermon, believing the greatest sermon was that of actions, not words. His men admired him greatly, and they never questioned his word or command. Their obedience wasn't created by a fear of punishment; it came from a desire to make Ishar proud, and to bring honor to the regiment.

    Buta turned to his left and regarded the deep shine of Daya's rifle. Buta admired Daya's work and, comparing it to his own, scrubbed much harder, taking care not to bend, bump, or bruise the end of the barrel. He scrubbed harder and harder, then turned to his right side and regarded Jivan's rifle. Buta sighed miserably, then turned to the soldiers and watched them mutilate the sandbags.

    After some time, Daya stopped scrubbing and admired his rifle. He stood up and moved out of the island of shade into the deep sunlight. Breaking the silence, he declared, "Look at this rifle!" He held up his rifle to Gurmukh, Buta, and Jivan. It reflected a fierce sunbeam into Buta's eye.

Buta shielded his eyes from the sun with his arm and thought about his sun spectacles. He said, "Hurts my eyes it's so clean!"

Gurmukh added, "So clean I could probably signal with it!"

Daya peered down at his rifle, transfixed by its ingenuity. For the others, it was merely an upgrade from the musket. But for him it was a marvel of engineering. Its barrel was two times larger at the end than the dated musket. It was much quicker to load, far safer, more powerful, and much more accurate. Unlike the musket, it fired without leaving much residue in the barrel, and it rarely left a thick, black cloud of smoke hovering about the sniper. Rarely did it obscure the battlefield.

After a moment, Daya went through the features of the rifle as though he were a salesman. "Length? Five feet. Weight? 8 pounds. Bayonet?" He fixed his bayonet to the rifle. When the bayonet was securely attached, he appraised it and said, "Three feet." He ran a finger across the blade and unintentionally sliced his finger. "Sharp. Razor sharp." He regarded the drop of blood at the tip of his finger in the sunlight, then returned his attention to the weapon. "Quick. Safe. Easy to load." He placed the stock under his right arm and pulled the lever back. He tipped the rifle downward, filled the chamber with a precise measure of gunpowder, loaded it with a ball, then turned the guard to remove any surplus powder.

Suddenly, a powerful voice startled him.

"Daya!" Ishar said, stepping up behind him. "What is this? What are you doing?"

All eyes turned to Ishar.

"Sir?"

Ishar took several steps toward him.

"What is this?"
"Sir?"
Ishar circled him. Faced him.
"Rifles are capricious weapons…"
"Yes, sir."
"If they are loaded, they must be fired. Or else they will not work when you need them to."
"Yes, sir."
Ishar studied Daya for a long minute, then pointed to a tin can perched on top of the stone wall. "That," he said. "One shot."
"One shot?"
"One shot."
"Yes, sir."
In one swift movement, Daya took aim, fired, and sent the can soaring through the air.
Ishar smiled.
"You're still my best shot."
"Thank you, sir."
Ishar turned and observed a pile of wooden beams by the barrack room. He ordered Daya to help him move a few beams closer to the entrance of the outpost. Another intuition.

Gurmukh and Buta marched toward the signaling tower located just above the barrack-room. As they passed the butterfly, Buta stopped suddenly and held his breath. He couldn't believe his eyes. Before him, a dozen ants pushed and poked and bullied the butterfly as it fought weakly and desperately with the last of its strength. Without flight or strength, it was helpless.

Gurmukh stood behind him and peered over his shoulder. He regarded the scene, and shook his head sadly as he witnessed an almost perfect line of a hundred shiny black dots marching toward the butterfly with one single intention - to devour it. He looked to the ants, then to the butterfly, then back to the ants. Finally, he said, "Not a good sign, Butaji. Not a good sign at all…"

Buta turned and shot him a stern look..

Gurmukh sighed and continued his march toward the signaling tower, leaving Buta hovering over the poor butterfly, somewhat distraught and unsure if he should interfere again. And just as he was about to enter the barrack room, he thought he heard something in the distance. Far off, he thought he heard the faint tremor of tribal drums. A cold shiver ran down his back. He froze at the entrance and turned slightly to gaze above Buta, beyond the outpost wall. He pricked up his ears and listened.

Nothing.
Silence.

All he could hear was Buta desperately apologizing to the butterfly for his fatal mistake, and a few soldiers drilling not too far away.

Slowly, Gurmukh turned and entered the barrack room. He walked to the back, looking out of the crude, sunlit windows as he passed them. He then climbed the creaky wooden steps up to the signaling tower and entered the tiny room. He placed his leather

Jessi Thind's Saragarhi

case on a small wooden table and looked through the window toward Fort Lockhart. After a moment, he lowered his eyes to the courtyard and watched Buta as he observed the butterfly, a thick ball of shiny black dots staggering back and forth with the last of its will.

Gurmukh heard another faint sound of tribal drums and froze just before completely assembling his heliograph. He peered intently at the horizon, searching. For what, he did not know.

Gurmukh stared at the empty land for a long minute. He looked down to Buta, who now watched the limp and lifeless butterfly being carried off by a dark cloud of ants. When he looked back up, his heart slammed against his chest. On the horizon, he spotted the silhouette of a man on horseback.

He narrowed his gaze.
He waited.
He pricked up his ears.
Listened.
Carefully.
For what, he wasn't quite sure.
But he thought he could hear the distant tremor of a million men on the march.

Buta watched the butterfly being dragged away to the feast. With a sigh, he looked up to the signaling tower and saw Gurmukh, frozen, staring at something way off in the distance. He did not know what to think, but Gurmukh looked as if he had just seen a ghost. With one last glance at the butterfly, Buta turned and quickly made his way to the barrack room. He marched through the narrow entrance, over the ancient floor, and climbed the creaky stairs. He stepped up behind Gurmukh and whispered, "What is it?"

Gurmukh answered without taking his eyes off the cavalryman.

"I don't know."

"You look like you've just seen a--"

Suddenly, Buta spotted the silhouette.

Peering over Gurmukh's shoulder, he felt a strange feeling inside. He heard the distant rumble of a million anxious feet on the march. A moment later another cavalryman appeared, then another, and still another. Soon there were a dozen cavalrymen staring down at Saragarhi. The tremor of feet grew louder and stronger as a massive dust cloud began to veil the cavalrymen.

Soon they could see nothing but dust.

They both tried to see through the veil.

Wondering.

Waiting.

When the dust settled, it unveiled thousands of tribesmen standing behind the cavalrymen. It was as if the mountain had suddenly opened up and an army of darkness had marched out.

The scene was beyond their capacity to comprehend.

They had never seen so many tribesmen.

Gurmukh stopped breathing. His heart lurched into his mouth and he watched in mingled awe and disbelief as this massive army marched toward them.

    Buta's mind would not accept what his eyes were seeing. He stared beyond the walls and blinked.

    Blinked.
    Blinked again.
    And again.
    Opened his mouth.
    Said nothing.
    Couldn't say anything.
    Didn't know what to say.

"Pathan! Pathan!" Buta yelled, rushing out of the barrack room into the courtyard. "To arms!"

All eyes went to him, then to the havildar.

Ishar rushed up a wooden ladder and gazed through a rifle opening. Seeing the massive army closing in on them, he turned to his men and gave quick orders.

Soldiers raced to reinforce the door with wooden beams, crates, stones, and sandbags. They rushed along the wall, found their positions, and waited by their rifle holes.

Buta, Daya, and Jivan took their positions on a ledge by the entrance. From their rifle hole they watched ten thousand men marching toward them in perfect ranks with several cavalrymen leading the way, a massive dust cloud gathering behind them. Each soldier in the regiment witnessed this and murmured a quick prayer.

At once, the marching stopped.

The drums ceased.

The dust settled.

Silence reigned.

A long breathless moment followed as the regiment stared into the eyes of some terrible beast of war. Suddenly, the chieftain kicked his black stallion to a full gallop and raced toward Saragarhi. He halted several yards before the outpost. His stallion neighed and shifted nervously, sensing the nineteen barrels directed at it. Sensing doom. The chieftain took a moment to calm his stallion, then he called out to the regiment:

"Sikhs of the 36th regiment! Why die for the British? Why die for a tyrant? Lay down your arms and surrender. You need not lose your lives for some meaningless fort. You need not lose your lives for politicians thousands of miles from here. Lay down your rifles, surrender, and we will spare your lives. You have my word."

All eyes went to the havildar. Two soldiers next to him

searched his face for marks of fear and uncertainty and found none. In their leader's eyes was the courage and strength of his ancestors. They knew instantly there would be no surrender.

The chieftain waited a moment. When no answer came, he shook his head in disappointment, reared his horse round, and returned to his army.

Buta watched as the chieftain worked up his army. He said, "What is he doing? Doesn't he know…?"

Daya glanced at him. "Know what?"

"He is already defeated."

"He is?" Daya asked.

Jivan turned to him but said nothing.

Buta's grin blossomed into a smile. "Yes. He is. We will quash every attempt they make on us. We won't even let him get within ten yards of the door. We will kill a few hundred, and we will leave him with such a bad taste in his mouth for fighting Singhs, he will run…he will run with his army wagging between his legs. You will see."

The chieftain called out an order. The tribal drums roared and the army stirred to a steady march. Ishar called out to his men, "Here they come!" He raised his hand and ordered that they should wait until they were closer, much closer. "Wait…wait…wait for them…"

The regiment watched as the army went from a steady march to a quick jog.

"Wait…"

The army approached and the drums roared louder. The chieftain called out an order. As if connected by one mind, every man went from a quick jog to a hard run. In the signaling tower above, Gurmukh watched the scene below and flashed a detailed account to Fort Lockhart. With his eyes on the army, Ishar raised his hand higher so that every soldier could see it.

"Wait…"

The chieftain gave another quick order. The tribal drums bellowed like a mighty dragon. The tribesmen raised their swords like deadly scales.

Ishar took in a deep breath.

"Wait…"

The dragon roared and shrieked and was on them at full charge.

"Wait…wait!"

Daya gazed and murmured to himself, "All falsehood has left me. My soul, my breath, my body and mind belong to Truth. My faith is in you, O Lord of the universe…"

The chieftain barked a final order. The dragon shrieked furiously and lunged for the door. Ishar yelled as loud as his lungs would permit:

"Fire!"

A deafening explosion roared through the outpost as nineteen rifles fired as one.

Jessi Thind's Saragarhi

An instant later nineteen tribesmen fell like sandbags.
Not a single ball was wasted.
Ishar yelled, "Fire at will!"
Nineteen thumbs scrambled to pull out cartridges.
Hard, calloused fingers quickly reloaded.
Sharp eyes gazed down the sight of the rifle, narrowed to slits, and aimed.
Steady, confident fingers pulled triggers.
More tribesmen fell.
And fell.
Daya shot a cavalryman off his horse. Jivan shot a drummer. Buta stood, peered over the wall, and shot a wild-eyed tribesman attempting to climb over. Nearby, a few tribesmen had already scaled the wall, but soldiers were bayoneting them and kicking them off the wall like children playing king of the mountain. None managed to clamber over. Below, the tribesmen kneeled, aimed, and fired long, unsteady muskets. They hit stone or air, obscuring their vision and adding to the cloud of gunpowder smoke that grew with every shot fired.

As the battle waged on, the chieftain surveyed the outpost and saw that his men would soon be crippled by their own musketry. But before he could say anything, something caught his eye. A glimmer of sunlight. He narrowed his eyes on the signaling tower. He waited. Nothing. As he was about to turn away, he saw it again, and again. When the signals ceased, he turned round and saw flashes from Fort Lockhart. At once he ordered three tribesmen to mark the signaler. They nodded their obedience, aimed their muskets at the tower, and commenced
firing.

Without interruption or intimidation, Gurmukh continued to maneuver his heliograph with the ease of a scribe using a quill. He signaled the happenings of the battle as tribesmen fell to their stony graves, spilling incredible quantities of blood at the entrance, creating a thick red carpet.

Despite the musket balls shrieking by his head, Gurmukh continued unflinchingly. He didn't falter once. He didn't miss a beat. Not even when a ball grazed his neck and sent a stinging sensation down his back. The only time he stopped was when a huge black cloud obscured his vision, making it impossible to see anything below. It was the darkest cloud he had ever seen. He could see nothing through it. All he could report were the cries of the dying, the drums of war, and the muskets firing through the darkness of pure day.

Suddenly, Gurmukh heard a bugle, followed by a desperate cry to retreat. A moment later he heard Ishar ordering the regiment to cease fire. Through the musket smoke, he glimpsed with disbelief the retreat of the mighty dragon. Even with its ten thousand claws and razor sharp teeth, it could not defeat a lion a millionth its size.

It was an impossible thought.

An impossible sight.

An incredible feeling.

Buta leered at Daya and Jivan with a victorious smile. They breathed heavily, and streams of perspiration dripped off their noses. Their foreheads, turbans, and poshteens were darkened by dust and residue. Buta laughed and said, "I told you. Kill a few hundred and he will run with his army between his legs." He laughed again and mopped perspiration off his face with his sleeve.

Daya ignored him, looked to the heavens, and said a small prayer.

Jivan gazed out of the rifle hole. "It's not over," he said flatly, and repeated the words again to himself. "It's not over..." He looked to the heavens and, like Daya, said a small prayer.

A soldier peered at Ishar's arm. Blood gushed out of a small hole in his poshteen. It streamed down the sleeve, dripped off his fingertips, and colored the gray wall with drops of red. It wasn't long before Ishar felt eyes on him. He turned to the soldier and asked, "What is it? Are you okay?"

"Me, sir? Not me, sir. Your arm…"

"Yes," Ishar said without looking at it. "I know. I can feel it."

The soldier went to his aid, but Ishar jerked his arm away. "See to the others," he commanded. "You can take care of this later. It is but a scratch."

"But, sir--"

"I'm not dead yet!"

"But--"

"Do as I say."

"Yes, sir."

As the soldier scurried down the ladder to aid the wounded, Ishar turned to another soldier and gave him an order. "Count the dead. Collect their rifles, munitions and provisions…and place them in the barracks. And make sure to load the rifles."

"The barracks?"

Ishar turned toward the barrack room. "If reinforcements do not come," he said in a low, pensive tone, "that is where we will make our last stand."

The soldier followed Ishar's prophetic gaze. "Yes, sir," he said, and climbed down the ladder.

Ishar watched him climb down, then looked up to the signaling tower. He lifted his rifle and, with his bayonet, flashed Gurmukh.

Jessi Thind's Saragarhi

There was no answer.

Again, he signaled the tower.

Still no answer.

The black cloud of war slowly dissipated. The silence and the sun returned, and the regiment could see that the entire army had fallen back to their ranks and lines. Gurmukh gazed out at the scene incredulously. He stared in disbelief at the dozens of dead tribesmen scattered before Saragarhi. Then he looked to the horizon at the dark and slow approach of the buzzards. He felt a terrible pang in the pit of his stomach. These scavengers were always an awful sight to him; they had always filled his heart with a terrible dread he could not name or understand.

A sunbeam assaulted his eye, jerking his attention to the courtyard. A glimmer of sun bounced off a bayonet, asking him when reinforcements were coming. When Ishar lowered his rifle, Gurmukh acknowledged him, saying he would soon find out. Gurmukh turned toward the horizon and relayed the question to Fort Lockhart. After a long, breathless moment, they flashed back that they were not sure, that they were doing their utmost to send reinforcements, but all paths to Saragarhi were blocked by the enemy.

When Gurmukh relayed the message back to the courtyard, Ishar sighed deeply and turned slowly. He looked to the tribesmen, to the buzzards in the sky, then to his men. He wondered how long they could keep ten thousand tribesmen from swarming the outpost. He turned his attention to a soldier walking somberly though the courtyard, carrying four canteens and rifles over his shoulder. He counted the canteens and registered the number in his mind as the soldier disappeared into the barrack room. He turned to his rifle hole and gazed out at the enemy. Deep inside, he knew the regiment could not hold this dragon off for much longer. Now they were only seventeen. Seventeen against one of the biggest dragons he had ever seen in his life.

The sun continued to pound its relentless fists against the tiny outpost. In the shimmering sky, several buzzards circled hungrily over the bodies, waiting for the men to leave so they could feast in comfort and safety. One impatient buzzard swerved up, then swooped down and landed beside the sun-baked body of a tribesman. It edged cautiously toward the body, watching the lines for signs of an attack.

The buzzard nudged an arm with a talon and shuffled back quickly. It eyed the body suspiciously for a long careful moment. It approached again, nudged the leg, shuffled back and waited for any sign of danger. When nothing happened, the buzzard approached the body confidently and went to peck a morsel of flesh from the blistering face.

As soon as the buzzard pinched the cheek, the seemingly dead body gasped to life with a start. A weak hand swiped the dark scavenger away. Before the startled bird could take to the sky to join its friends, a musket ball pierced the bird's crown, making it pay for its impatience. The chieftain lowered his musket and watched as his soldier dragged himself toward him.

In the outpost, a soldier loaded his rifle and took aim. But Ishar stopped him. "No!" he commanded.

The soldier seemed confused. "Sir?" he questioned.

"You heard me," he said. "Let them see to their wounded. He won't be fighting again...not today...not for a long time."

"Yes, sir."

Another soldier turned to Ishar and made a quick observation.

"I doubt they would show us the same compassion."

Ishar watched the tribesman drag himself through the dust, leaving a dark trail of blood.

"We are not them."

"Yes, sir."

Buta, Daya, and Jivan watched as the tribesman dragged himself, inch by inch, toward his army.

"He won't make it," Jivan said. "He's lost too much blood."

"He'll make it," Daya said. "I'm sure. He'll make it…"

Jivan shrugged. "If you say so…"

Buta regarded them both with an inward smile. For a long, breathless moment they watched the tribesman move across the ground like an ancient turtle, a wounded turtle. They watched him with the wide, desperate eyes of gamblers, though neither had ever gambled in their lives. They watched him until he couldn't drag himself anymore. They watched him turn on his back, wheezing. He let out a cry that cut through the silence like a knife. The sun burned into his soul like acid. He saw the buzzards circling above. Slowly, his eyes shut. His heart stopped…and all went black.

Daya sighed.

Jivan grinned.

Buta wiped his brow and took out his canteen. He took a long swallow of refreshing water and savored the moment like paradise. He would have continued if Jivan hadn't put a hand on his canteen and said, "Careful with that. We don't know how long we'll be without reinforcements." Jivan fixed his gaze upon the army. After a moment, he added, "I think they will try to wait us out. They know we are low on provisions."

"You think we scared them?" Daya asked, peering through his rifle hole, examining the thousands of tribesmen standing restlessly in the sun.

"I think we surprised them," Jivan answered. "I do not think we scared them. I think they will attack again--"

"And we'll kill another hundred, and then they'll run," Buta interrupted.

Daya asked, "What are they waiting for? Why don't they just attack?"

Jivan gazed out at the bodies, then the army. "They're playing on our nerves," he said. "They think some of us will break down with time. It is an old trick. They know that idle men talk. They know that men faced with such odds have the tendency to despair. They are hoping to use our own thoughts against us. That is what they are doing. They are hoping our fearful thoughts will weaken us…exhaust us. They are hoping our thoughts will destroy us before their blades do. They are hoping our fear will lead to an easy surrender."

Buta snickered. "They can hope all they want!"

Daya added, "There will be no surrender."

Jivan nodded in agreement. There would be no surrender. And there would be no words or thoughts of despair. What the enemy failed to realize was that the Sikh heart was woven out of the immortal threads of timeless stories - stories of awesome endurance, courage and martyrdom. Nothing emboldened them more than being brought to the brink of annihilation. Survival was more than an instinct; it was in their every limb, muscle, and cell. It was in their blood. Centuries of persecution had put it there.

"Surrender!" Buta said with a hearty laugh. "Us? Now why would we surrender? We're not the ones who are outnumbered." Jivan wiped a drop of sweat from his nose and grinned for the first time in hours. "We're not outnumbered?" he asked, turning to Buta, who winked and said, "No. We're not."

A white, burning sun oppressed the sky and threw daggers of heat upon the outpost. The air was hot, dry, and painful to breathe. It had been several hours since the first attempt on Saragarhi, and each soldier stared out at the enemy, wondering when the next attack would come, wondering when reinforcements would be deployed. Water was running low. Patience, lower.

Buta had been inspecting and scrutinizing his poshteen for some time. "You know what I would like?" he said, breaking the silence. "A different kind of poshteen. A special kind of poshteen. One…that can stop a musket ball."

Daya scrunched his eyebrows. "A poshteen that can stop a musket ball?" he asked.

"Yes. That is what I said."

"Ridiculous."

"Why do you say so? Why is it ridiculous?"

Jivan listened but said nothing.

Buta said, "I wouldn't mind having a poshteen that could stop a musket ball. I think that would make me feel a lot safer."

"Me too. But such a thing could not exist. Such a thing is not possible."

Buta shook his head. "What is possible and what is not possible is dictated only by the limits of the mind."

"It is not possible," Daya added. "Not unless it is made of stone, and I would not be one to wear a poshteen made of stone in battle. You would lose all your energy just lifting your arm. Think about it…you would kill yourself by walking."

"You will see," Buta said. "One day all the Queen's men will wear my poshteens." He paused for a moment, imagining his poshteen. "First, I will buy hundreds of ordinary poshteens," he went on. "Then, I will layer them with…with…well, not stone, but something light and impenetrable."

Jessi Thind's Saragarhi

Daya laughed absurdly. "Yes, Butaji. But that is it. What will you layer it with? What is that something?"

Buta narrowed his eyes and thought for a long, difficult moment. Then he shrugged and said, "I don't know. Not yet, anyhow. That 'something' is a mere technicality. But when that 'something' comes to me, it will be miraculous. And when I know what that something is, I will sell the idea to the Queen, and all the Queen's men will have to wear my poshteens, and I will become a very wealthy man, and with my wealth, I shall gift humanity with hundreds of miraculous ideas, because my mind is big and free and connected to something even bigger, something immeasurable and indefinable; and it is, I assure you, unfettered by negative thoughts like, 'it is not possible.' I will invent it. The 'something' will come to me. You will see."

Jivan indicated the ten thousand tribesmen with his rifle.

"Not if they have anything to say about it."

Buta's voice sharpened.

"They are nothing! Look at their numbers. Look at ours. If they were anything, we wouldn't even be talking right now. That's what I think. You will see. Reinforcements will come, and when they do they'll run like hyenas from the lion."

Jivan peered out at the army, and watched thousands of swords and lances reflecting sunbeams in every direction like a giant diamond. Staring at them was like traveling back to a time when invasions from Afghanistan and the mountain tribesmen were endemic, a time when his ancestors not only had to protect their land and goods from these ruthless invaders, but also their families, their lives, their way of life-their faith. Hundreds of thousands of Sikhs had fallen under the great red sword of religious intolerance. Thousands upon thousands had been ordered to renounce their religion, and when they refused, they were gruesomely tortured in forts, in villages and in markets. And always, the tortured one would remember the Almighty, and he would recite powerful words and hymns, and the words, like a million invisible butterflies, would lift his consciousness to a place where pain did not exist, and no possible torture could harm him.

Countless stories of impossible courage and endurance in the face of overwhelming odds and religious persecution were in the hearts of every soldier of the 36th regiment. It was in the way they spoke, the way they related to one another, the way they listened to one another, and in the way they stared at the enemy without the slightest thought of retreat or surrender. A strong, powerful history infused the regiment, and if there were brief moments of despair, they were quickly annihilated by a story remembered.

Daya took a deep breath and felt he was living something out of one of the many stories his parents had told him growing up. "This is not unlike the story of Bibi Dalair Kaur," he said plainly.

"Is it?" Buta asked, unsure.

Daya turned to him and asked, "Don't you know the story of Bibi Dalair Kaur?"

"No," he answered. "And I don't have a family protection shabad either."

Jivan listened to his comrades without interrupting.

Daya thought for a long moment, then he began to tell the tale as he remembered it. "I forgot the details," he said. "But...I remember she and her warriors were surrounded in a fort like us, and they were severely outnumbered by the Mughals."

"And were they all killed?"

"Yes, but they were victorious, for they never surrendered or begged for mercy."

Jivan waited for more, but Daya didn't continue. Realizing this was the extent of his story, Daya sighed heavily and shook his head in grave disappointment. "That doesn't do justice to such a great story. I'm not sure many tellings would, but I can assure you, that does not do justice to the story of such a great and noble warrior. Your parents may have told you the tale, but whether you were listening or not is another issue. It cannot be that this was all they told you."

"It is what I remember."

Jivan snapped at him. "Yes, and I am sure you know quite a few British stories by heart and in much greater detail." He sighed. "Forget your stories... Soon, my friend, you will forget who you are and you will only know British stories; that's all you will memorize and learn, because that is all you will value."

Daya cringed at this, but didn't respond for he saw another tirade in Jivan's eyes.

Shaking his head, Jivan sighed and gazed out at the chieftain. After a short, reflective silence, he told the story of Bibi Dalair Kaur.

"The Mughal imperials had completely surrounded Fort Anandpur and had, for days, demanded that those inside surrender and renounce their faith, or else fall by the sword and be delivered to hell. But those lionesses inside the fort would rather die than insult their ancestors by surrendering to those who, for centuries, had wanted nothing more than their extinction."

Jivan paused a moment to let these words sink in.

"These brave women had always lived for Truth, and now they would die for the very Truth they had upheld all their lives. They could not embrace religious intolerance, gender inequality, and a caste system that weighed and valued people like the British do now with their scales and instruments. These brave women would not be intimidated by death. Truth does not need fear of death or hell or promises of paradise. Truth, you understand, needs no rhetoric… Truth needs no sword to make it true."

Jivan paused again to collect his thoughts.

"And with this understanding, Bibi Dalair Kaur and her warriors laughed at these soldiers who tried to entice them with promises of paradise and intimidate them with threats of hell. They swore they would rather die a hundred painful deaths than surrender to them. They would not become slaves, nor cooks, nor cleaners, nor concubines, as these men had surely intended. Nor would they run helpless into a blazing fire and commit a strange act in the name of honor. No. They would use their kirpans as kirpans were meant to be used. In defiance of the tyrant. To protect the poor. To empower the helpless. And never…never for the tyrant's greed."

Jivan turned to Daya and studied him for a long moment. He turned to Buta, grinned, then returned his gaze to the army.

"They would fight. They would fight like the lionesses that they were and had always been brought up to be. And in fighting to their inevitable deaths, they would achieve an honor worthy of all those who had fallen to the Mughals and the Afghans before them. And, in this way, Truth would prevail. They fought not to avoid death but to fulfill a desire to make their ancestors proud. And so, the Mughals, still ignorant to the fact that they were battling women, fired their cannons at the wall and stopped only when they had succeeded at creating a breach. Upon discovering that women garrisoned the fort, the Mughals roared with laughter."

Jivan gazed at the sky and shielded his eyes against the piercing white light. He returned his gaze to the army. He saw the chieftain examining the outpost, searching for any weakness in the wall.

"When the exaggerated laughter ceased, the general, tall, powerful, built like a wall, yelled his frustration at being up against a contingent of women. Then, in dawning horror, he realized…these women not only opposed him, they were defeating him! For a moment he gazed at all the dead Mughals scattered around him like slaughtered sheep. Then, unable to contain his anger, he cursed and reprimanded his men as though they were lower than dogs. Of course, Bibi heard all this from the fort, so in front of all his men she challenged him to a duel."

Jivan paused with the realization that his story was a measure different from the one his mother used to tell him growing up. He searched his memory for the exact details as they had been related to him. Not finding them, he continued the story as his own:

"The general stepped forward with a few men and made derogatory jokes against women in a failed attempt to hide the terrible fear of losing to a woman. In fact, so great was this fear that it helped Bibi in ways she didn't quite understand. But the fear was there; she sensed it, and she beamed at him gloriously as he approached the breach. She acted like a child who was eager to play-fight with him. As he walked through the damaged wall, he made elaborate gestures to his men, telling them that this would all be over very quickly and effortlessly. And it would be…but not in the way he had anticipated…"

Jivan paused, turned to Daya, then Buta. He raised his eyes

to a buzzard, and watched the bird soar across the sky for a moment. He looked back toward the army, but imagined Bibi Dalair Kaur withdrawing her kirpan with a mighty ring that resonated through the chambers of his mind.

"The Mughals and lionesses encircled the two leaders, and the deadly duel ensued. A moment later, the general was on the ground, headless, his neck spitting and sputtering blood, his every limb shaking violently. Horrified, the Mughals, who had accompanied their general into the fort, went to arms and they were, as you can imagine, just as easily beaten. Some say it was an event comparable to feeding mules to lions."

Jivan turned to Buta. He scrutinized his face and could see his eyes were brighter and stronger, despite his exhaustion. All effects of the heat and sun were momentarily gone. Jivan hesitated a moment to let the images take root in their minds.

"Well, the other Mughals fell into a quick retreat and would have run away had they not been halted by one soldier who had kept his focus throughout the ordeal. But this soldier was a coward, and instead of fighting Bibi and her warriors in hand-to-hand combat, he wasted the emperor's munitions by ordering incessant cannon fire and gunfire in a barrage he thought no living being could survive."

Jivan paused for dramatic effect. He could hear the cannons blasting through his mind. He could see the cannon balls ripping through the walls and the fort collapsing into a huge mushroom cloud of dust.

"When he had succeeded at pounding rubble into dust...he sent in a few thousand soldiers to inspect the remains. There, they found the bodies of the lionesses covered in dust and rubble, their eyes shining brilliantly like precious black pearls of courage, of strength, and of sacrifice. It was as if their souls demanded their broken and unresponsive bodies to stand and deliver a few more blows to the enemy. That is the story as I remember it."

Buta's eyes were wide and alive with the story. He turned to Daya. "Sorry, Dayaji, I like his version better."

Daya nodded. "Me too."

Buta thought about the story a moment. "Although, I think I'd like it better if the enemy had just retreated...or perhaps it would have been nice if reinforcements had come to relieve them."

Daya grinned.

"Yes. That would have been nice, too. But you can't change history."

Jivan snapped.

"Yet tyrants do all the time."

Daya's eyes dimmed. He didn't want to get into it. He didn't want to say anything that would provoke another tirade. He already knew Jivan's opinion on history, and how he believed it was used not as education, but as the tyrant's final weapon to demean, weaken, and destroy a conquered people's esteem and self-concept so they would be easier to control and subjugate. He looked out at the enemy, and he watched a buzzard swoop down and land beside a corpse.

"Don't forget your history," Jivan said to Daya in a voice full of accusation. "You are your history. Remember that. Always remember that. That is precisely why books are burned and then rewritten, that is why--"

"I haven't forgotten my history!" Daya interrupted.

"Your stories as well..."

Daya sighed but didn't answer. He watched the buzzard edge closer to a body. A musket fired, missed the bird by hairs-

Jessi Thind's Saragarhi

breadth. It took to the sky in a hurry.

Jivan added, "You need not exterminate a people physically to exterminate them absolutely."

Buta thought about these words but didn't quite understand his meaning. Even though Daya shot him a searing look to keep quiet, Buta said, "You need not exterminate a people physically to exterminate them absolutely.' What does that mean?"

Jivan turned to him. "Exactly what it means," he replied, "that it is always better for commerce to exterminate people inwardly rather than physically. Always. And all you need to do is exterminate what makes those people who they are. "

"How do you mean?" Buta asked, wanting to hear more.

Daya looked away, trying not to listen. He watched another buzzard try its luck. It landed beside a corpse and edged closer and closer; with the roar of a musket, it vaulted to the sky to rejoin its friends.

Jivan leaned closer to Buta.

"Make those people feel like their way of life is inferior to the Anglo-Saxon way of life; fill them with profound insecurities and make them reject their culture for a culture that is foreign, hostile, and most unfamiliar to their hearts. One that is shallow, empty, intolerant, and all about possession, acquisition, consumption; but one that is also very polite and invisible, even political, one might say…with its greed, hate, and cruelty."

"I've heard this before!" Daya interjected.

"I haven't," Buta countered.

"Did you know the British were the very first to exterminate entire communities that wouldn't be destroyed inwardly, and did so with plague--"

"Yes," Daya answered.

Buta's eyes grew wide with interest. "I didn't know that."

"It is true. And yet, in their books, they make every other people seem like savages. But really, to be fair, only a savage would unleash a plague on entire communities."

Daya snickered. "It can't be proven."

"You are right," Jivan admitted. "It can't be proven. I only know what I know from other soldiers. The Irish. The Scottish. The Welsh. All of whom, I assure you, have interesting tales to tell you about the British, tales that won't be remembered a hundred years from now, tales that didn't quite make the books."

Jivan laughed as if this were absurd.

"It's true. What I am telling you can't be proven, and you can be sure it will likely never be proven. It will never be proven because those who unleashed the germs also control the evidence. And in the future, they will control the historians that will use this evidence to build their books, prove their history, and construct their theories. And they will succeed at stacking a lie on top of a lie, proving a lie with a lie, constructing a lie with a lie. Nothing more than–"

"So we should trust nothing, then. Is that it?" Daya interrupted.

Jivan ignored his comment and looked straight into Buta's wide eyes.

"No one will question history because it will be validated by reports based on events observed through their eyes, written by their officers, their scribes, journalists, and professionals. And it is precisely this evidence and not history that will need to be scrutinized. Because when you pile dung on top of dung, you've still got dung, only it's bigger and messier--"

"And smellier!" Buta added, and he laughed at the image the words invoked.

But Jivan hadn't meant to be amusing. "This is how they hide their savagery," he continued, when Buta cleared his throat and was quiet again. "They erase the memory of it, or perhaps we can say they hide it in a heap of dung that no one dares rummage through."

Jivan paused to look to the sky. He wiped his wet face with his sleeve and fixed his gaze on the land. Another impatient buzzard swooped down and landed beside a corpse to feast. It inched right up to the body. It gazed at the army to one side, the outpost to the other. On both sides, it felt the promise of certain death. It waited breathlessly until it could wait no more. It went for some flesh. As soon as it went to snap at the corpse, a musket ball ripped through the air and leveled the dark scavenger.

Jivan watched a thick black feather float to the ground. He took a deep breath and turned to Buta. His tone grew fierce against the injustices swarming through his mind.

"They who would not cut up the land, who would not squander their natural resources, who would not make a religion of consumption paid the highest price."

Buta leaned closer, deeply interested.

"The highest price?"

"Blankets."

Buta grimaced. "Blankets?"

Somehow he had not expected this answer.

Daya's face paled from what was being said. They were things he simply refused to believe about those he felt had brought order and infrastructure to his country.

"Blankets," Jivan assured Buta, who couldn't believe what he was hearing. "Blankets and little tin containers of plague gifted to the elders after peace negotiations." He paused to indicate the now-stirring army with his rifle. "Believe me, one of those blankets is a hundred times more lethal than the men you see out there. And what you see out there is a lot easier to fight. And that is the truth."

Buta felt sick to the marrow that the British would use germ warfare against entire communities.

"Your truth," Daya said, turning to Jivan.

Jivan shrugged. "I'm not here to argue with you over what has or hasn't been told to me by others."

"By others," Daya said. "Rumors, exaggerated half-truths at best."

"Perhaps. Perhaps you are right."

"Then why speak as though you are speaking truth. You speak as though these things really happened. And yet, there is nothing to prove they did those things, save what a few disgruntled Irish sepoys told you in passing. So say what you will, but remember, it is your truth and not mine."

Jivan nodded. His voice fell to a grave whisper. He turned to Buta. "As the rumor goes," he said with a measure of sarcasm, "one blanket could and did exterminate entire communities. And those few who did survive were placed in reservations and made to ingest a great lie specifically engineered to erase the memory of who they were, what they stood for, and who the true savage is." He turned to Daya. "My truth."

"Yes. Your truth."

Jivan turned to Buta.

"Exterminate a people's songs. Exterminate their stories. Exterminate their history. But do not exterminate the living, breathing person. Culture alone is quite enough to conquer an entire people for centuries without prolonged physical force or threat. Cultural genocide is the way of the clever tyrant, and it is something the British excel in because they need loyal consumers to purchase all those useless products they manufacture with our stolen resources."

Jivan paused. His throat was hoarse, dry and cracking. He grabbed his canteen and took a small sip. He wet his lips and continued:

"We didn't get the blankets, because we would cut up our land, we would pay their taxes, we would sell our resources at a pittance, and we would purchase our own resources in the form of useless products."

"You sound ridiculous," Daya blurted out. "You can say what you want, but I just think you sound ridiculous."

"Listen here, Dayaji, do you actually think the British are here to stay?"

"Yes. I don't see why they would leave."

"Commerce," Jivan said bluntly.

"Commerce," Buta repeated, and shot Jivan a perplexed look.

"They are following an old Roman formula that says one does not need to occupy a country to control it, so long as one controls the few who govern and influence the masses. It is much too expensive for them to keep their army here. It will take them fifty or sixty years to have complete control of our politicians, historians, and our teachers--"

"Ridiculous!" Daya interrupted.

"No, not ridiculous. It will take them fifty or so years to defeat us within so that the next generation will seem Indian on the outside, but will be so empty and insecure about their identities that they will not know who they are and will constantly and unconsciously seek the Master's validation, and that validation will come from overseas. My truth."

Daya grumbled his disagreement. "You just cannot see the good of being part of an Empire. You cannot appreciate the order and the law and the institutions they have brought us."

Jivan thought about this for a moment. "You are right," he agreed. "There is good. There are benefits. But the ends, Dayaji, the ends never justify the means. Never. And the means…well, they were of a true savage. Means that will be forgotten in time."

Daya sighed and turned from Jivan.

"The next generation will only learn about the good of the British, never the crimes or atrocities to our people, or any other people for that matter. Civilization according to the British, written by insecure, brown hands, who will write while guided by the invisible hands of the reward-giver, the validator, the Master."

"You should be a prophet, not a soldier."

"That's true," Buta said with a broad smile. "That's true…"

Jivan ignored this comment. "You will see," he continued. "They will leave, and the new generation will be plagued with an unspoken disease of British needs and desires, and brilliant Indian minds will compete against one another for British rewards, British luxuries, British degrees, and this control, like the plague blankets, will be impossible to fight because it will be invisible."

"Your truth!"

"Yes. My truth."

Buta grinned and said, "You're both a little bit right. There is a little good, and there is a little bad."

"Time will tell the tale, Dayaji."

"You just cannot see the good."

"You will see," Jivan said. "You will see."

Buta indicated the enemy with his rifle. "Not if they have anything to say about it."

Jivan took a moment to observe the enemy. Thoughts

swelled inside him like an ocean, and he needed to release them or he would burst. After a short silence, he opened his mouth as though it were the valve of his mind.

"Pens controlled by brown hands will write a white man's history and will be made to do so for credibility. They will use our own scholars and scribes to distort and write down their lies and half-truths, their version of what happened here."

He went quiet for a moment. His eyes fixed on Daya's kirpan, and he wondered if the British would forever respect, revere and tolerate the kirpan that so bravely and gallantly defended His Majesty's Empire.

"And who will contest what our own scholars write? Anglo-Saxon history cloaked and validated by the Indian. A history that will forever afford the British the image of the great civilizers of the world. Because, you must understand, if we are made to remember their crimes and atrocities against us, there would never be any commerce between the Indian and the Englishman. Never. And commerce is everything for them."

Another silence. His eyes turned to the sun. It was surely the fiercest sun that had ever blazed in the sky. His mouth was parched and his throat was burning. But there was nothing he could do for his thirst. He needed to conserve his water. He needed to make it last for however long it took for reinforcements to arrive. He turned back to Buta and continued, his voice blunt, stern and unapologetic.

"And this great betrayal by our own intellectuals will forever seek white rewards: medals in battle, awards for books, novels, poems, and scholarly work, and honorifics to place by our names. You name it, they will control it, directly or indirectly. So where the Afghan once threatened our existence by the sword, the Anglo-Saxon now threatens it by the pen; and the pen, Dayaji, is and always will be mightier than the sword."

"Your truth."

"Yes, my truth," Jivan said, looking into Daya's eyes. "You don't need to accept my thoughts or opinions, but please, I beg of you, ask yourself if the original people you so adamantly would like to join still exist."

Daya turned to him, curious. "I don't understand."

"You should understand there is a reason, a very dark reason, they have so much land to give away."

"I don't understand."

"You don't understand? Or you don't want to understand?"

"I don't understand!"

"Then understand this: paradise land once thrived with countless religions, civilizations, and temples. And now, I ask you...where are those religions? Where are those civilizations? Where are their sacred buildings and temples?"

Daya's blood boiled. He gave Jivan a searing look and turned away. He obviously knew the answer but didn't want to say it or hear it. Buta had a strong feeling he knew what Jivan wanted to hear. Daya often spoke with abhorrence against the Afghan for the alleged extermination of the Buddhists. Now, Jivan spoke of another great extermination with the same revulsion. Only he wasn't talking about the Afghan. He was talking about the British. And the thought of them using billions of invisible soldiers to invade and infest and eat away the bodies of women, children, and the elderly shattered his perfect picture of his glorious Empire. Realizing Daya was ignoring him, Jivan answered for him:

"I believe you put it very nicely before...what was it you said? Oh yes... Destroyed! Desecrated! Eliminated! And the remains have been dusted under a dirty carpet they politely and correctly call a 'reservation'."

Jivan paused at the sudden din of a rousing dragon. The clanging of swords, the stomping of feet, and the shouts of the chieftain as he inspired death, brutality, and merciless slaughter in his men. He looked out from the rifle hole and said, "Yes, Dayaji, I know. My truth. My truth of those you so thoughtlessly revere."

He waited for Daya's reaction. When he said nothing, he added, "They often call the people they eliminate 'savages'. But truly, if a savage defines you as a savage, perhaps you are the civilized one."

Jivan waited.

Daya said nothing.

Jivan watched as the chieftain galloped toward the outpost. He watched the chieftain approach and knew he should save his energy, but he had more to say. "So go ahead," he said in flat tone. "Take that land. But let us hope that countries do not carry karma like people. Because if they do...I wouldn't claim a single handful of dirt from that land. You want my truth. You want my point-of-view. That land is destined to be lost in the same way it was acquired."

Jivan fell quiet. He listened to the hard gallop of an approaching stallion. Abruptly, the galloping stopped. A short silence followed. The chieftain broke the silence, calling out to the regiment with his usual rhetoric.

"Sikhs of the 36th regiment, be reasonable. Look around you. Look! Have you ever seen so many warriors? Why lose your lives for the British? Why lose your lives like worthless pawns in a white man's chess game? Be reasonable. Look around you. You boast yourselves valiant sons of Guru Gobind Singh. Yet you fight for one of the greatest tyrants the world has ever known. The whites have taught me in blood and cruelty what they are!"

He paused and waited for a response. When none came, he

added, "Sikhs of the 36th regiment, this is not your fight! It is not. And neither I, nor any of my men, will ever stop as long as one white man remains on our land. If you do not give reason to this affair, I will not, nor will any of my men, show you mercy. Sons of Guru Gobind Singh, be reasonable. Lay down your arms. Surrender. Surrender and we will spare your noble lives."

    The chieftain waited a long moment. When no answer came, he shook his head in disappointment, gritted his rotten teeth, and quickly returned to his army. The tremor of drums began, and the ground shook under the march of the mighty dragon. Gurmukh quickly flashed a message to Fort Lockhart, letting them know the tribesmen were beginning to mount their second attack, and that water, ammunition, and reinforcements were badly needed. In reply, they signaled that all pathways were still blocked by the enemy, and that they would have to make do with what they had for the time being. For how long, they did not say.

"Fire!"

Ishar bellowed.

Fifteen rifles fired as one. Fifteen tribesmen fell like sandbags, and not a single cartridge was wasted. The second attempt on Saragarhi had begun. Thumbs, fingers, and eyes worked as one.

Thumbs, fingers and eyes worked tirelessly and endlessly as desperate tribesmen charged the door and walls. The regiment was beginning to wane. Many tribesmen had managed to climb into the courtyard. They rushed to the door to let their comrades inside.

Ishar saw men pulling and tugging at beams and crates. No one else had noticed them. Without a moment's hesitation, he rushed to meet the threat. He slid down the ladder and charged with long, impossible strides. In one single movement, like a flash of light, Ishar slashed two men with his bayonet and emptied his barrel in the last man's face. Then he turned and saw another tribesman drop into the courtyard. He charged at him at full speed, despite his aching and exhausted muscles.

The tribesman lifted his musket and aimed it at Ishar. As he fired, Ishar ducked, heard the ball shriek over his head. Swerving so that the tribesman could not track his movement, Ishar leaped to the wall and ran three feet across its stony surface. As his boots skidded downward, he jumped off the wall and aimed his bayonet at the stunned tribesman. The tribesman saw the glitter of sun reflecting off the bayonet just before it plunged through his neck, ending his life.

Picking off cavalrymen like tin cans off a wall, Daya shot a tribesman off his horse. He pulled out a cartridge with his blistered and bleeding thumb. As he reloaded, he murmured, "All falsehood has left me. My soul, my breath, my body and mind belong to Truth." He lifted the rifle and aimed. "My faith in you, O Lord of the universe..." He took a moment to breathe, then shot another man straight off his horse.

Buta peered over the wall nervously, and shot any tribesman attempting to climb over. Beside him, Jivan shot at the three men firing at Gurmukh, picking them off one at a time. Even when he missed his mark, he hit someone or something. They were everywhere.

Suddenly, three tribesmen dropped into the courtyard like thieving bandits in the night. Without seeing Ishar, they fixed their gaze on the door and rushed to open it. Ishar quickly reloaded his rifle and charged like a lion toward a herd of gazelle. As the tribesmen attempted to remove the last few beams, one saw him coming. He turned to face Ishar and went to shoot him. Ishar aimed his rifle as he rushed them and was the first to fire. The tribesman's legs buckled and he fell with a smoking ball lodged between his eyes.

The other two tribesmen turned to him. Another raised his musket and aimed. Ishar's free hand went for his quoit. He extended his arms back, took a second to aim, and flung the sharp iron disc with all his strength. The quoit whirled through the air and reflected white sunlight in every direction. A second later the tribesman crumbled to the ground, his finger on the trigger, scalped at the crown.

The last tribesman let out a terrible war cry and attacked Ishar with a long, curved sword. Ishar parried with his rifle. He moved left, right, backward, forward. The tribesman leaped toward him with a snarl, his sword held high. He swung it with all his strength. Without thinking, Ishar maneuvered to evade the blow. The tribesman hit the hard ground. Vibrations shot up the sword, stunning him. Ishar spun around him and thrust his bayonet into the tribesman's side. Before the tribesman fell to his death, he swiveled wildly and thrust the hilt of his sword against Ishar's head. Black dots swam in front of Ishar. His knees buckled and he collapsed with the sun glaring down on him.

No one fired at Gurmukh anymore. He looked down and watched his comrades kicking and bayoneting tribesmen off the wall. One of his comrades had been shot. He was slumped over the wall. Dead. Another soldier fought on the wall. He lost his footing and fell directly into the jaws of the dragon. A swarm of tribesmen closed in on him like fangs. Gurmukh's hand clenched into a fist as he watched them brutally stab, swipe and hack away at the soldier's every limb.

It was a gruesome sight.

Gurmukh closed his eyes, took a deep breath and collected himself. He opened his eyes and unclenched his fist. He forgot his despair and flicked and jerked his instrument again, asking when reinforcements would be deployed.

Ishar tried to keep his eyes open. It was of no use. He sensed this might be his time. He heard the din of battle all around him. He felt the warmth of blood oozing down his face. He felt the heat pounding him. Beating him. Choking him. His lungs rasped for breath. His eyelids grew heavy like stone.

They opened, and they closed.

Opened.

And closed.

He heard the call of the bugle.

The retreat.

The last thing he remembered was smiling.

A violent shake and a taste of water returned Ishar to full consciousness. He slowly opened his eyes and saw a soldier tending to his wound. "I'll take care of it," Ishar said stubbornly. "Look to the others…see to me after…" His voice trailed off. He still felt drowsy. He reached for the soldier's canteen and took a long pull of warm water.

The soldier grimaced as he appraised the wound. "Sir," he said after a moment, "It is bad…"

Ishar's forehead had been split to the bone. "You heard me!" he said in a weak, yet kingly tone.

"But…"

"I am not dead yet. I will be fine. Tend to the others."

"There aren't any."

Ishar gave him a look.

"There are no wounded…only…"

"How many?"

"Seven."

Ishar sighed deeply. He surveyed the fort, taking everything in at once. The soldier bandaged Ishar's forehead with a thick cloth generally used for turbans. The smell of death filling the air made him nauseous. Ishar collected his wits and gestured toward the door. "Take two men…reinforce that door. They will return."

The soldier nodded obediently. "As soon as I am done with you," he said. "You're not dead yet, but you will be if I leave this open. You give the orders. I keep you alive so that you can continue to give the orders."

"I didn't say anything."

Sunbeams descended on the outpost like blades of fire. Ishar shielded himself with his arm. The air stung and was hot and heavy, making it difficult to breathe. He had never felt so weak and dehydrated in his life. He took another swallow of water. Then another.

And another.

An instant later, his canteen was empty. The soldier unhooked his canteen from his belt. He handed it to Ishar, who refused it and told him to conserve his water. The soldier reminded Ishar that his job was to keep him alive so he could continue to lead the men, and that he wouldn't survive much longer without water. Ishar knew the truth of his words. He nodded, took the canteen, and swallowed a mouthful of water as if it were amrit.

"I can't believe it," Buta said, staring out at the enemy. "So many, and still they cannot take Saragarhi." He shook his head in disbelief. After a moment, he added, "We will be given medals for this. I am sure."

Jivan shook his head at the thought of medals.

"Perhaps," Daya said. "But if reinforcements do not come soon, they will be pinned on our dead bodies."

"They will come," Buta said. "I am sure of it."

Jivan looked at a buzzard tearing away morsels of flesh from a corpse hidden behind a shrub. He instantly thought of the British in India.

"They'll give you a medal, Butaji, and then they'll use your medal to glorify fighting and killing for the Queen. Then, a century from now, they'll use that same medal to convince young Indians to spill their blood for pot-bellied politicians, fighting wars that have nothing to do with them. Perhaps they will even send our future young ones back here. Only our young won't be defending as we are, they'll be invading and robbing people of their land and resources. It will be a shame to see young Sikhs putting on the same masks as those who once tried to exterminate them."

Daya sighed heavily, but said nothing.

Buta turned to Jivan and asked, "Is that a prophecy, prophet?"

"It is merely what I think."

"Sounds like a prophecy. You would have made a good prophet."

Daya quickly grunted his agreement. Then he turned to Jivan. "And why, pray tell, invade Afghanistan?" he asked. To him, this was nothing but an absurdity, the conspiracy talk of old men; it was the talk of those who think they have figured out all things and everything in the world, and spend their days lecturing at teahouses and dhaabas.

Jivan snickered hoarsely. "Why invade Afghanistan? Well, why invade and occupy India? Same reasons, Dayaji. Same reasons. Commerce. Resources. They will want to do to Afghanistan exactly what they have done-and are still doing-to India now. They would invade now, if they could. But they can't. They are overextended now. They lack the human resources to take it all in one fell swoop. So they have to wait until they are controlling India from overseas before they can even consider invading Afghanistan."

Jivan gazed to the horizon, to the mountain range. "If you must know, we are not here to protect our land as they make us think and believe. We are here to make sure the Tsar does not get Afghanistan before they do. To make sure the Russians do not get Afghanistan before they do. That is why we are on the frontier, not to protect India as they would have us believe."

Buta couldn't believe what he was hearing. He shook his head and laughed. "What taverns do you frequent, my friend? I must know. I really must know! I could fill a hundred journals with your conspiracies. Then a hundred more!"

Jivan paused and looked through the rifle hole at the enemy. Then he turned to Buta and shook his head.

"Believe me, they don't want the Russians here. They don't want the Tsar to have his commerce and language here, and they don't want the Tsar to have any easy routes to Persia. It's simply a matter of commerce."

Daya gasped at this. "Don't your lips get tired? My ears do!"

"A hundred years! You will see. Time will reveal the truth of my words. If they can keep the Tsar out, they will be back here, and they will invade using already-conquered soldiers. Our young.

Our children."

"Your truth."

"Yes, my truth. Rumors. Believe what you will, only know that if you are given a medal, never for a moment believe it is for you. It is for them. It is for the Queen. To bait our young."

Buta's eyes dimmed at this. He shot Jivan an unexpected frown. He opened the valve of his mind and said, "I am sorry, but I do not think like you. And though you are welcome to your truth, I will not let you make me feel guilty for wearing a medal if ever I should be-and I should be-honored with one, especially if I should ever wear that medal while telling my grandchildren stories."

Daya fixed his eyes on Buta. He never knew medals meant so much to him. "Neither would I," he said confidently. "Neither would I…"

"In fact," Buta added, "I would wear mine proudly."

"And so would I!"

"We all have our own truths," Jivan said, not quite understanding what had triggered Buta.

Buta lowered his tone. "We clearly do," he agreed. He thought a moment. "Unlike you, I don't believe in cultural genocide. I don't. I have heard your arguments with curiosity and interest, and I just don't think it can happen the way you say it does, nor do I believe the British would wipe out entire communities with plague-infested blankets. I don't. I think that is preposterous! I listen to you and I say nothing because it is interesting and…well…I just don't believe we are losing our culture as much as I believe we are constantly reinventing who we are in a world that is forever changing."

Jivan interjected. "I think-"

"Let me finish," Buta interrupted. "I listened to you without interruption, now I would like to say something and I expect the same."

Jivan nodded.

"There is no conspiracy against the Sikh. There isn't. All cultures take and borrow from one another. That is the way the world is. That is the way Waheguru intended it to be. And we shouldn't be scared of losing who we are, nor should you be suggesting that this is something we must fear. There is no plot to muddle our history...our stories...our identities. The turban and kirpan and kara will forever be respected in the Empire. And as far as the Empire is concerned, I tell you we are equal subjects. We are. And no dominion can deny us this truth."

Jivan listened attentively.

Buta looked to Daya, then turned back to Jivan.

"We are equal subjects with the same rights and privileges as white subjects. And he will go to this dominion, and he will get free land like any other white subject, and he will not be disenfranchised."

Daya nodded at this.

Jivan hoped he was right.

Buta continued after a moment's reflection.

"Life is changing, and we will have to change according to life. That is all there is to it. That is the way it is. This doesn't mean we lose who we are. It only means we will have to reinvent ourselves, and do so without losing our essence, our stories, our history. We are equal subjects and we have as much to offer the English as they have to offer us."

A reflective silence fell upon the three soldiers.

Suddenly, there was a noise.

They looked at one another.

There was another noise.

The sound of stone breaking.

Crumbling.

They listened intently for the sound of movement beyond the outpost. When Buta craned his head over the wall, he saw a tribesman trying to dislodge stones from the wall. Buta stood slowly and quietly. He aimed his rifle. Pulling the trigger, he ended the man's life. At that very instant, a musket roared. A ball shrieked by Buta and he lost his footing. He staggered left and right, and just before he fell out of the outpost, Jivan lunged forward and caught his hand, holding Buta over the wall.

Buta felt exposed.

Terribly exposed.

He struggled to pull himself up.

Jivan struggled with him.

A musket ball blasted the wall right next to his chafed and bleeding hand. Dust and stone fragments burst all over him.

Now he felt spotted.

He sensed the eyes.

The musket barrels.

He heard the roar of muskets and he felt the dust and stone blasting all around him. It covered his turban, his face, and his beard.

Daya stood, exposing himself to a hailstorm of musket balls. He bravely reached over and grabbed Buta's other arm. Daya and Jivan struggled desperately against their own dehydration and exhaustion. They pulled and panted and fought for breath. Their hearts beat like thunder as they yanked and heaved against the threat of death looming over them like buzzards.

Jivan stopped pulling for a second.

Just a second.

He closed his eyes.

He searched for something nameless within.

Deep within.

With every ounce of strength he had left, he heaved with a loud, desperate cry, and pulled Buta straight over the wall.

Buta panted heavily and calmed his heart. Safe on top of the wall, he let out a sigh. He lowered his feet to the ledge. When he went to crouch to safety, one last musket ball nicked the top of his turban and propelled him forward. He lost his balance. Once again he staggered on the shaky ledge...and once again, he fell. Only this time, he fell into the courtyard.

Ishar heard a loud thump, followed by a groan of agony. He turned to the courtyard and saw Daya and Jivan rushing to aid Buta, who lay in a pool of his own blood, clutching a broken shinbone.

Ishar hastened to Buta's aid. He hurried down the ladder and reached him in three strides. He looked to the bone jutting out of the kurta, unraveled a few feet of his turban and tore the piece in two. He scrunched one piece into a ball and placed it in Buta's mouth, telling him to bite down. He prepared to wrap the other piece around the leg so he could shift it back into place. He moved to the leg. Jivan and Daya glanced at each other, then looked to Buta with the ball of cloth in his mouth.

Ishar tore the kurta so that he could see the wound. He inspected it and looked to his men. They watched in horror, but said nothing. Without warning, Ishar turned back to the leg and snapped the bone back into place.

A terrible crack resonated through the outpost, followed by Buta's muffled screaming. Each soldier closed his eyes for a moment, as if feeling their comrade's pain. Silence returned and Ishar placed the knife by the bone for strength and support. He wrapped the leg tightly and securely.

Jivan swallowed a hard lump.

Jessi Thind's Saragarhi

Daya, too.

A terrible silence reigned in the outpost.

All eyes looked upon Buta as he bit the ball of cotton down to his teeth and tears of impossible agony ran down his face. When the leg was properly secured, Ishar, Jivan, and Daya carried Buta to the shadowy barrack room. Ishar ordered Jivan and Daya back to their positions. They nodded silently and saluted their havildar. Then they turned and marched toward the blinding light that poured through the door like a river of gold.

Before Jivan reached the door, he stopped. He turned to Buta and gazed at him for a long moment. Then, he saluted his friend as if he were the king of England. Daya turned and did the same.

Buta's eyes watered with a profound realization: he might never see his friends again. This was their last moment together. He swallowed an impossible lump. He took in a deep breath and forgot the terrible pain that shot up his back like a flaming spike. With wide, glassy eyes, he returned their salute, holding his hand by his crown a moment longer than usual. His friends turned on their heels and marched out of the shadows and into the sweltering courtyard.

Ishar grabbed a rifle and detached the bayonet. He turned to Buta. "Can you move?" he asked.

Buta took a few steps forward with difficulty.

Ishar handed him the rifle. "Use this for support," he said, eyeing his leg.

Buta held the butt of the rifle with his torn fingers. He took a few steps forward using it as a walking stick. "Yes," he said, holding in his pain. "I can move."

"Good! You're not dead yet."

"No, sir. Not yet..."
"Good! I still need you!"
"Yes, sir."
Buta took a few more cautious steps.

Ishar smiled and nodded proudly at Buta's effort. Ishar then indicated the pile of rifles and said, "Make sure they are all loaded. You watch the wall from these windows." He pointed at the three openings in the room. "Any milk-livered Pathan pokes his head above the wall, you know what to do."

"Yes, sir," Buta said with a smile. He gazed at Ishar and was struck by the calm in his eyes and the strength of his expression. His strength filled the room like the sunlight pouring through the windows. And his courage filled Buta's heart and made him feel invincible. He had never respected a havildar more, and he thought about how fortunate he had been to serve him. He turned to the square pools of light and held his busted ribs. This morning he had wished to see action. He had received much more than he had bargained for.

Ishar shuffled toward a window and was about to give him more instructions when suddenly, they were interrupted by a voice that thundered from beyond the walls of the outpost. Beyond the walls, the chieftain called out to the Sikhs:

"Sikhs of the 36th regiment! This is your last chance! Lay down your weapons and save yourselves."

He waited for a response or any sign of surrender. None came.

"Care to know what will happen if we catch you alive? Care to know what torture and suffering awaits you for your insolence? You cannot even begin to imagine what I will do to each prisoner we capture alive. You don't believe me? You can ask the few Russians who have already tried to make this land their own. How long did they last? Not long. And how long do you think you can hold the outpost? How long? Not much longer, I am afraid. Not much longer, I promise. Such a shame! Brave, brave sons of Guru Gobind Singh wasted for fat political tyrants sitting merry and smug thousands of miles away. Hear me now: Lay down your weapons, or I will personally skin you alive and hang you at the gate for the crows!"

The chieftain waited a moment, his eyes red with frustration. When no answer came, he gritted his teeth, clenched his fist, reared his horse round, and returned to his army weaving and winding around the bodies of his fallen men.

Gurmukh watched the scene below from the tower. For a moment he felt a flash of awe and disbelief. Over two hundred dead bodies of the enemy were scattered around Saragarhi. He suddenly felt like a character in an epic poem. After a few seconds, he brought his thoughts back to the moment. He leveled his eyes to Fort Lockhart and signaled that the enemy was once again preparing to attack.

Below, Daya took in a deep breath. He knew there would be no reinforcements. He could no longer fool himself. He was living the last moments of his life, and this fact stirred up something strange within him, a gentle tug in his heart. He turned to Jivan and held his gaze, without knowing or understanding what his heart wanted him to say. "Prophet," he said at last, still unsure about his words. "You are...I mean...despite our differences...what I mean to say--"

Jivan didn't let him continue. His heart understood. He embraced his comrade and said, "Brother, let me say this...despite everything, I thank Waheguru...for every ridiculous, pointless argument we have ever had!"

"Me too, brother," Daya murmured, "me too..."

"Imagine if we had thought alike. Imagine how that would have been!"

Daya agreed with an unexpected laugh. "Yes! That would have been boring."

"Though you know, let's admit, I am and have been right about everything!"

"Yes, prophet, if you say so."

There was a short silence. Jivan held Daya's gaze. Finally, he broke the silence, saying, "It has been a great honor, my friend."

"Yes. It has been a great honor, prophet. A great honor."

When they separated, they turned to their rifle holes and gazed out at the dragon. Jivan watched with curiosity as the chieftain ordered his men to prepare torches. He narrowed his eyes to pensive slits. "What will they do with those?" he asked, almost to himself. Then he gazed to where an overfed buzzard suddenly took flight. A thick, dry shrub answered his question.

The cavalry charged ahead while the infantry waited behind, patiently. They approached the outpost and halted a few yards away. They regarded one another, then fixed their eyes on a bush or shrub. They aimed carefully, and lobbed their torches into the air. A moment later, tiny imperceptible fires grew into long daggers of flame. Ishar swallowed as the smoke rose to obstruct their vision. He knew they would no longer be able to guard the door, and he knew it wouldn't be too long before they would have to retreat to the barrack room.

With thick flames crackling all around him, Daya aimed his rifle at a cavalryman who had still not thrown his torch.

"All falsehood has left me…"

The cavalryman raised his torch.

Streams of smoke began to obscure Daya's vision.

"My soul, my breath…"

The cavalryman held his torch high above his head, preparing to lob it.

The streams came faster and thicker.

"…my body and mind belong to--"

Suddenly, there was a loud crack.

Several explosions.

Hundreds of muskets fired at the outpost.

And Daya's head slumped lifeless over his rifle.

Jivan swallowed.

"Dayaji?"

He knew.

"Dayaji?"

He sighed heavily.

He breathed slowly, in disbelief.

He put his hand on his friend's shoulder. Closing his eyes, he murmured a small prayer. He opened his eyes and gazed at his friend for an endless moment, giving his final respects, thanking him inwardly, saying goodbye. Somehow, Jivan still felt his presence. Much stronger than before. He shook himself back to the moment and fired his rifle faster, much faster than he had ever fired a rifle before. The flames had spread along the wall and had completely covered the outpost in a thick black veil that seemed to be woven out of tar. He could still see, barely. He coughed and covered his mouth with his hands. Perspiration mixed with smoke and covered his entire face with a thin film of sludge.

A bugle sounded, rousing the mighty dragon. They heard the thundering footfalls of ten thousand men on the advance. A roar louder than a volcano cut through the smoke. Not one soldier could see anything through the veil of tar that stung their eyes and filled their lungs. The dragon charged. The soldiers fired desperately into the darkness. Then, suddenly, the dragon surged against the door and wall. The entire outpost shuddered against the impact.

A few tribesmen removed some stones from the wall. They pulled and pushed and kicked in an attempt to dislodge and weaken the wall, to create a breach large enough for a man to walk through. Ishar felt something in the pit of his stomach. He turned toward the courtyard, stared at the wall. Smoke slithered out of the small hole they had made. His heart almost stopped. He had to stop them before they widened the breach. Without a moment to lose, he slid down the ladder and stormed toward the small hole while the other soldiers fired helplessly into the black void.

Ishar was too late. By the time he reached the smoking hole in the wall, tribesmen, blackened by dust and smoke, surged through the breach with swords raised and ready. Ishar lunged forward like a lion and struck one, two, three tribesmen in one deadly, flowing movement. He took position by the breach and cut down every tribesman that tried to enter his kingdom. He piled their bodies one on top of another, filling the breach with a wall of flesh.

The door swelled and creaked. Part of it splintered. Jivan looked to the door uneasily. He watched the swelling, listened to the creaking, the pressure of thousands upon thousands pushing, kicking, screaming for his death. He calculated it would burst any moment now. A sudden grunt brought him back to the moment. When he looked up to the wall, a tribesman veiled in smoke towered over him with his sword raised. Jivan raised the barrel of his rifle and fired.

Just in time.

The ball ripped through the tribesman's jaw, tooth, and tongue, sending him back into the thick, black, smoky void. Another tribesman clambered over the wall, and Jivan reacted just as quickly. He shoved the butt of his rifle in the enemy's gut, then thrust his bayonet into his thigh. Kicking the tribesman off the wall, he turned to the courtyard. Ishar guarded and blocked the breach like an iron wall of blades, piling bodies strategically, obstructing the breach, making it harder and harder to get through, and easier for him to kill anyone who made the attempt.

Jivan tracked the movement of a tribesman about to attack Ishar from behind. He grabbed Daya's loaded rifle. He only had one shot, one chance. He narrowed his gaze. He concentrated. He aimed as best he could through the darkness. He fired. But at that very instant, a thick stream of smoke obstructed his view.

He stopped breathing.

His eyes strained though the darkness.

His head craned upward, but he couldn't see anything.

Only when the smoke eddied away did he see the tribesman lying dead on the ground as Ishar continued to build his wall of bodies.

He breathed with relief. Distracted, Jivan was not aware of the threat looming right behind him. In the moment he had taken to help Ishar, a tribesman had climbed the wall, snuck up behind him, and raised his sword high above his head. The tribesman was now about to let the blade fall across the back of his neck. A sudden explosion from the barrack room saved him. When Jivan turned round, all he saw was the tribesman falling backward into the darkness. Before he could think about his next move, he heard creaking again. Louder. The dragon roared. Fiercer. He turned toward the entrance.

The wooden door burst into a thousand splinters and made an opening big enough for two men to walk through at the same time. Ishar yelled for his men to leave the wall and cover the entrance. He turned back to the breach and thrust his bayonet through a tribesman's gut. As he removed his bayonet, three other tribesmen fell toward him from behind. In a blur of motion, Ishar turned and swiped two with his bayonet, then crushed the skull of the third with the heavy butt of his rifle.

Within seconds, Jivan and two other soldiers were guarding the door, employing the same strategy Ishar used. Every dead tribesman was a building block for a wall. Behind the wall of flesh they could hear the dragon roaring, threatening to burst through the outpost to destroy everything and anything in its path. The soldiers didn't allow what they could not see intimidate them. They focused on one tribesman at a time. Sometimes two. Sometimes three.

Two other soldiers flanked their havildar.

Ishar acknowledged them with his eyes, then turned, and evaded a large, curved blade that swished by his head and clanged against the wall. The sword vibrated out of the tribesman's hand. Ishar lunged forward and plunged his bayonet into his ribcage where it lodged. For an instant, he locked eyes with the dying man.

Jessi Thind's Saragarhi

Ishar tried to jerk his bayonet free, but it was of no use. The bayonet was stuck in bone. When another tribesman charged him, Ishar gave up, released the rifle, and withdrew his kirpan. He parried wildly with his attacker, and leveled him. But as one attacker fell, three others appeared. He did not think. Had no time to think. He maneuvered and shuffled across the ground, and fought with pure instinct. All three soldiers defended the breach as one. They struck, lashed, and kicked as if linked by the same mind, the same heart, the same soul. When one moved, another leaped and struck. When one backed away, another lunged forward and swiped. When one turned to parry a blow, another protected his back.

They were one.

Tactically.

Mentally.

Spiritually.

Their strategy worked brilliantly; a large pile of bodies now obstructed the breach so that only two or three tribesmen could infiltrate at a time. For now, the breach was not a threat. The real threat came from the men hidden by the smoke who clambered over the walls.

Jivan felt the sword coming before he saw it. He ducked, spun, and plunged his bayonet through his attacker. He withdrew his bayonet, heard a footfall behind him, swiveled, and lunged at another tribesman, cutting him down like a blade of grass. He heard men, thousands of them, on the other side of the wall, nervous, anxious, frenetic, clambering over each other, climbing the wall. He loaded his rifle and surveyed the top of the wall. He shot one man, reloaded, shot another, and another.

Suddenly, Jivan heard a wail.

A gasp.

He turned fast.

Jessi Thind's Saragarhi

Seven tribesmen were on two of his comrades.

He didn't have time to figure out where they had come from.

He fired his rifle and leveled one tribesman. He felt something ancient move through him, seize him. Without knowing how, without intent or understanding, he unsheathed his kirpan, grabbed another from the ground and became a whirlwind of annihilating power, reflecting sun and shadow in every direction, sending each man to his hard stony grave without mercy or hesitation. He fought faster than he thought. Faster than any man could track. Like he spoke. Direct. Bold. Unforgiving.

For a brief moment, Jivan stood motionless, panting heavily, drenched in blood, gazing at a pile of corpses scattered around him. He couldn't believe he was still standing. Neither could his comrades. As soon as they thanked the Almighty for their incredible speed, the enemy pounced on them again, their blades reflecting light and shadow. They parried and swiped and lunged, and the enemy crashed down on them, wave after wave. They leveled as many as they could. But there were far too many, and they were coming from every direction.

In the barrack room, Buta rushed from window to window, firing endlessly at tribesmen who clambered over the wall in the thick smoke as they poured into the outpost like a dark, poison stew. He was a machine of speed and accuracy. There was no pain. His pain wasn't even a thought. Not even an afterthought. Something powerful and nameless flowed through him so that he forgot his broken leg, his busted ribs, and his chafed hands. He was unstoppable, and he moved as if he were completely whole, stopping only once to look at Ishar.

He had never witnessed such a scene. And knowing these were the last moments of his life, he knew he never would again.

Ishar's kirpan sliced and crunched through flesh and bone, and he moved in ways no human should have been able to move. He fought with impossible strength and agility, despite heat exhaustion and dehydration. And for a brief moment, Buta forgot where he was, who he was, and he felt he was watching a living myth.

But Ishar was no myth.
He was real.
Human.
And a tribesman had proven it.
Buta saw the tribesman attack Ishar from behind.
Ishar sensed the sword.
Turned.
Angled his kirpan.
A heartbeat...
Too slow.

And the tribesman slashed him at the stomach. Ishar fell backward, holding his gut.

Buta was shocked back to reality. He yelled his anger, aimed his rifle, and shot the tribesman down. Then he watched in disbelief as Ishar struggled desperately to stand and return to battle. He struggled against his torn gut and ripped shoulder and lifted himself up. Blood dripped from his kirpan. From his hands. From his mouth. From his nose. From his head. One hand kept his insides from spilling out. He staggered left, then right. He had difficulty hearing, keeping balance, seeing. He even had difficulty feeling. His limbs were numb with adrenaline. He staggered and fell backward again.

Buta watched, feeling helpless. He saw how desperately Ishar tried and tried again to stand and return to the fight. Then...Buta made a decision. He left his post and ran out to Ishar. He clutched him by the belt and dragged him back to the barrack room, where he gazed in disbelief at his wounded gut. A mess. A terrible mess.

Ishar continued his desperate attempt to stand, but fell back again and again

"Sir," Buta said, placing a hand on his shoulder, stopping him.

Ishar looked at him.

Buta indicated his stomach.

"Your stomach."

Ishar sighed. "Yes, I know. It feels bad..."

Buta nodded slowly, his eyes wide. "It is, Sir. It is bad..."

A short, almost fatal silence followed. Ishar looked to his gaping wound, sighed, and said, "Still not dead yet...not yet...we can get me up again..." He raised his eyes to Buta. His eyes grinned and held his gaze for a moment. He gestured to the rifles and ordered Buta to reload them.

Buta nodded and reloaded the rifles. Ishar unraveled a good length of his turban with one hand, holding his gut with the other. When he had the length he required, he ripped the cloth with his mouth. He looked to Buta and watched him reload the last rifle. "Help me," he said, and handed him the cloth. Buta quickly bandaged Ishar's stomach as he watched the window and doorway for signs of the enemy. A minute later Buta helped him up and handed him a rifle. Without another word, they were firing at the enemy side-by-side.

Thick black smoke rose to the signaling tower and filled Gurmukh's lungs. The deadly stew thickened and poured over the walls, filling the outpost with its darkness. He coughed and held his breath for a moment. He stopped signaling. He lowered his eyes to the courtyard, and through the smoke, he watched as his comrades outside fell one by one. He watched each man fall until Jivan was the last soldier standing. Jivan parried, lunged, kicked, and shuffled backward, unwittingly moving toward a wall. As Gurmukh watched this glorious scene, his eyes grew hot and blurry with tears.

Not tears of despair.
Something else.
Something inexpressible.
Something...
Sublime.
Even...
Divine.

Jivan played out the final act of a life that had been written long ago. Long before he had been born. And the performance was more than Gurmukh could bear. It was something he had only heard of in the stories of old. Something he had only dreamed about or imagined when, as a child, his parents and teachers had regaled stories of his ancestors.

Now the story was real.
Jivan was part of it.
He was part of it.

A wall stopped Jivan from parrying backward. Gurmukh's heart thundered with a sudden need to join him. His heart clenched to a stop when a swarm of tribesmen dropped from above and overwhelmed Jivan like ants.

Gurmukh breathed. He raised his chin and his eyes hardened. He grabbed his heliograph and signaled Fort Lockhart for permission to leave his station to confront the enemy. When he lowered the heliograph, he sensed something strange, something invisible near him. For an instant, just an instant, he felt Jivan's presence behind him, beside him, all around him, inspiring him, strengthening him, empowering him. He closed his eyes, and his heart acknowledged and filled with his presence. Gurmukh opened his leather case and dismantled his heliograph, gazing toward Fort Lockhart, eagerly awaiting permission to leave his post.

Despite the futility of the situation, Ishar's courage and calm demeanor did not falter. He moved with Buta from window to window, firing, reloading, firing, reloading, never letting up or giving in to the pain from his torn gut.

Gurmukh gazed toward Fort Lockhart intently until the answer came. He read the flashes on the horizon. Permission granted. He placed the dismantled instrument in its case. He opened his canteen and took a long, refreshing pull. He closed the canteen and placed it on the table. He mopped away the smoke and perspiration from his brow. Then he lifted his rifle from the table. Slowly, he loaded the weapon and attached the long bayonet. When the bayonet was fastened, he turned round and marched toward the steps.

Ishar and Buta took a moment to watch Gurmukh descend the steps with the peace and calm of a man about to fulfill his destiny. Slowly, he marched toward them and stopped. Saluted. Said nothing. His eyes embraced them both, then he turned round and marched toward the sunlit doorway. For a moment, he fixed his gaze on the chieftain closing in on the barrack room with dozens of frenzied tribesmen surrounding him, protecting him.

Still panting heavily, Buta and Ishar watched Gurmukh.
Watched him focus.
Watched him decide.
Watched him suddenly charge out the door.

Gurmukh rushed fearlessly toward the chieftain while everything around him disappeared. The sun. The sky. The buzzards. The mountains. The smoke. The fire. The broken wall. The corpses. Everything. All that remained was the enemy. Their swords, muskets and lances. The fight filled him, soaked him, became him. It was in his ears, nose, eyes, skin, sweat and saliva. It was in his arm, his hand, the finger that held the trigger. It was even in the cartridge, the powder, the ball waiting to explode from the barrel. He pushed through the enemy like a hurricane. He shot one tribesman. Bayoneted another. Flung his quoit at yet another. Then he withdrew his kirpan and cut and lunged and pushed his way toward the chieftain.

The chieftain shuffled backward and parried Gurmukh's every blow. But Gurmukh was outnumbered, completely overwhelmed by tribesmen. One slashed his leg, and he buckled to his knees. Another slashed his arm deeply and his kirpan fell in a pool of blood. No sooner did Gurmukh fall to his knees than the chieftain snatched him and bound him in a powerful headlock. Withdrawing a small, blunt knife he reserved for torture, the chieftain roared like a mad animal.

"You will pay for my losses! Your own screams will haunt your soul forever!"

He drove the knife into Gurmukh's back and twisted. Gurmukh bellowed and quivered in agony. He kicked and squirmed, trying to free himself from the chieftain's firm hold.

"I will make you suffer! I will hear you scream!"

The chieftain pulled the crimson knife out of Gurmukh's back and angled it against his neck.

Gurmukh's eyes widened. Though he never imagined he would fear death or torture, he fell into a desperate panic, kicking and squirming in every direction.

The chieftain pushed the knife into Gurmukh's flesh.

Gurmukh's heart thundered through his chest. He instinctively kicked the ground in a frenzy to free himself. Every cell of his being anticipated the culmination of pain and agony to come.

But then...he heard something that calmed him.

Buta's voice in the distance, reaching his ears between rifle bursts.
Hearing Buta's familiar voice, Gurmukh stopped, his eyes and lips still quivering.

Breathing heavily, Gurmukh listened...to the sweet sound of his family protection shabad. Buta recited it clearly, and the words floated in the air like a butterfly.

The chieftain made a face.

So did his men.

Gurmukh looked around him. As Buta continued to recite his protection shabad, Gurmukh could not see...but he began to feel. He could feel invisible eyes on him, just as he had in the signaling tower. He looked around and calmed himself, slowing his heartbeat to a stop. For long, extended seconds, images of Sikh martyrs and warriors flashed before him. Slowly, unbreakable courage replaced the natural fear of torture and death. In a second that seemed like eternity, a small grin broke over his face as he found within himself a place of calm, peace, and Truth. No one could touch him or harm him.

The chieftain stared at Gurmukh, amazed that he was now calm. Peaceful. Unbothered by the pain and the death to come. The chieftain looked down at his prisoner.

Gurmukh's eyes reflected the sun.
Two golden pearls.
He breathed slowly and deeply.
Waiting.
Breathing.
Slowly.
Deeply.
Waiting.
He didn't squirm.
Didn't kick the ground.
Didn't try to escape.

This was his death, the way he was destined to leave the physical plane of existence. He had lived his entire life with integrity and courage, and an unshakeable belief in something more, something greater, something grand and mysterious. Now he would not undermine the way he had lived or his belief in the Almighty by fearing the very end the Almighty had written for him. He breathed the stinging hot air. He felt the strong presence of something more, and, though he could not see them, he felt the strong presence of his ancestors all around him. Within him. In his blood. In his muscles. In his heart.

Gurmukh took in a deep breath. He thought about his grandparents, his great grandparents, and his ancestors. He felt a sudden relief. He smiled. They would soon be reunited. With this thought, he closed his eyes, and hummed his family protection shabad.

The chieftain's eyes widened.

Gurmukh's lips mouthed words as the tribesmen whispered curiosity and disbelief.

Suddenly, Gurmukh's eyes sprang open. Loud, powerful words of his shabab poured out of his mouth. The chieftain cursed him and cut into him with cruel ceremony, prolonging every measure of pain, needing this soldier to beg for mercy, for compassion, to beg for his comrades to come out and save him from his agony. But there was no agony. No pain. No begging. Though the torture was dark and incomprehensible, the shabad raised Gurmukh high above his condition.

The chieftain looked down into Gurmukh's eyes. Instead of the trembling fear of death, he saw only reflections of his own impotency. His own defeat. Even in torture and death, this soldier would secure a victory over him. The thought infuriated the chieftain. Drove him crazy. His every muscle tensed. His jaw locked. He gritted a rotten tooth to paste. He twisted and pulled and pushed the blade with cruel intent. He stopped suddenly. He pulled the blade a few inches away from the neck. A long, dusty finger extended into the gaping wound, probed and poked the artery. The finger hooked the fleshy opening and pulled and pushed and twisted. He was determined to hear this man scream and squirm like all the others he had tortured throughout his life. He would not be defeated. He would prolong the suffering for as long as it took to hear him cry and beg for mercy.

But Gurmukh did not beg for mercy.

Did not cry for a quick death.

Did not scream for the pain to end.

Did not…

Jessi Thind's Saragarhi

Feel pain.

Instead, Gurmukh's voice rose an octave with every useless movement the chieftain made. He cried out his family shabad, fixed his gaze on the sky and did not feel the stinging hot blade slicing through his neck. His eyes shone with the sun and his voice filled the outpost with victory. Words fluttered out of his throat like glorious butterflies, and those butterflies lifted his soul higher and higher into the spiritual realm of existence, to a place where there was no pain, and where he knew his ancestors were waiting. Waiting and watching.

For a moment, Gurmukh saw what he thought was a mirage. Around the tribesmen, shadows appeared and disappeared. They closed in on him. His shabad carried strongly into the barrack room and filled Buta's and Ishar's ears. They joined him and sang strongly and proudly with him, filling the entire outpost with their spiritual victory. All three soldiers voices' rose together.

Suddenly, Gurmukh saw a face in the shadows. He reached out to take a hand no one else could see. He cried his shabad as loud as his dry, exhausted lungs would permit, and he floated high above his pain, as if raised by the hand of the Almighty. Gurmukh's words turned to gurgles, his mouth sputtered blood, and he left his earthly body.

A long silence followed. Even the tribesmen were left speechless by what they had witnessed. The chieftain gazed at his knife and felt his defeat. He breathed heavily. He broke the silence with an order for a full attack on the barrack room.

Ishar and Buta fired at their attackers. Countless musket balls assailed the barrack room like a hailstorm. After a minute, the firing ceased. Ishar turned to see Buta lying on the ground with a hole in his neck.

Buta looked up at Ishar.

His eyes said everything his crimson mouth couldn't.

Ishar watched the life drain from Buta like a river into the sea.

And then...he was gone.

A loud thump returned Ishar's attention to the moment. He turned and saw a torch on the ground spreading flames across the wooden floor. He rushed to extinguish it, but the dry floor and a munitions crate had already ignited. He heard another thump behind him. He turned. Another torch. Then another. And another. The fire spread across the floor and engulfed him in flames and smoke. He didn't have time to fire a last shot.

Outside, the chieftain and his men watched the barrack room burst out in long blades of yellow and orange fire. Flames reflected in the chieftain's defeated eyes. This morning, he had expected to take the outpost in a single assault. They had fought twenty-one men from morning to late afternoon. The thought was impossible to register. Impossible. And he knew deep in his heart that this was no victory. It wasn't anything close to victory. It was one of his greatest defeats. Suddenly, a man burst through the flames.

"Bole Sonihal Sat Sri Akal!"

Ishar cut and sliced though stunned tribesman like crop before the reaper. He set others on fire with every movement of his flaming body. The chieftain grabbed his musket, charged the flaming warrior, and plunged the bayonet through his trunk.

But not even this could stop Ishar.

The chieftain stared in disbelief as Ishar raised his kirpan high and forced himself, one step at a time, through the bayonet, through the barrel.

Frozen, the chieftain didn't react. Couldn't react. Was frozen in terror.

With the last of his will, Ishar pushed himself all the way to the trigger. Blood dripped like a fountain from the barrel of the musket. The chieftain looked into Ishar's eyes and let go of the weapon. He gazed into his eyes and waited for the deathblow.

Before Ishar could let his kirpan fall, a tribesman shot him in the back of his head. An instant later, the chieftain snapped out of his trance and mopped Ishar's blood off his face. Still in a half-daze, he looked to the man who had saved his life and nodded in appreciation.

The chieftain stared at Ishar's smoking corpse as though it was a rare jewel. At last he tore his gaze from the corpse, turning round and round, gazing in disbelief at his surroundings. Nothing his eyes registered made sense. Gradually, his eyes dimmed with insult and shame. Profound shame. His face pale as death. The ground was broken and torn, and the dirt was thick, dark, and crimson with the blood of his men. Hundreds of them. The scene was beyond his capacity to accept. He swallowed hard. Then he barked an order for the outpost and every corpse to be burned to a cinder.

It took a little more than seven hours for an estimated ten thousand tribesmen to bring down Saragarhi. Early the next morning, reinforcements arrived only to discover charred remains of the epic battle. The tribal chief, ashamed of having lost so many men to so few, had the outpost destroyed and all the bodies burned. Only later would he admit the great loss he had suffered to Havildar Ishar Singh and his men. All twenty-one soldiers received a standing ovation from the British Parliament.

Within days of the chieftain's confession, the whole world knew about the battle. Each soldier received the highest military honor of the time: The Indian Order of Merit. No other contingent of troops in any military force, before or since, has been decorated with such an honor for a single battle. The battle is now documented by the United Nations as one of the most courageous actions in military history. A memorial in honor of these Indian soldiers stands at Saragarhi.

The Butterfly by Jay Singh

www.deshidtz.com

Free Yourself
Find Yourself
Be Yourself

ISBN 142512761-4

Printed in Great Britain
by Amazon